EVERYTHING CALLS
FOR SALVATION

Daniele Mencarelli

EVERYTHING CALLS
FOR SALVATION

*Translated from the Italian
by Wendy Wheatley*

Europa
editions

Europa Editions
27 Union Square West, Suite 302
New York, NY 10003
www.europaeditions.com
info@europaeditions.com

*This book has been translated with the generous support from the
Italian Ministry of Foreign Affairs and International Cooperation.
Questo libro è stato tradotto grazie a un contributo per la traduzione assegnato dal
Ministero degli Affari Esteri e della Cooperazione Internazionale italiano.*

Translation by Wendy Wheatley
Original title: *Tutto chiede salvezza*
Translation copyright © 2022 by Europa Editions

Library of Congress Cataloging in Publication Data is available
ISBN 978-1-60945-806-5

Mencarelli, Daniele
Everything Calls for Salvation

Art direction by Emanuele Ragnisco
instagram.com/emanueleragnisco

Cover design and illustration by Ginevra Rapisardi

Prepress by Grafica Punto Print – Rome

Printed in the USA

CONTENTS

To fighters
To crazies

EVERYTHING CALLS
FOR SALVATION

"I've lost my soul, Mary! Help me, my little Madonna!"
Black and more black. This must be death.

"I've lost my soul, Mary! Help me, my little Madonna!"

The stench of burning, increasingly strong. Heat, then fire, flames.

I thrust open my eyes at the world as if it were the first time. I barely manage to keep my lids up, just for a split second.

"I've lost my soul, Mary! Help me, my little Madonna!"

There's a stranger next to me. He looks like Francis of Assisi, but crazed, dirty, thin as a rail, with a lighter in his hand. The reek of burning is my hair. He is setting my head on fire. I want to call for help. But I can't. My brain is unable to communicate with the rest of my body.

A shrill scream, like a girl's, explodes into the air. I turn my head. It comes from the mouth of a forty-year-old man, hair dyed red, what little of it still grows, all flipped to one side. He screams again, "Pino! Pino! Madonnina is setting the new guy on fire!"

The nurse is a paunch on legs, all white. He pauses at the door, looks in. What he sees makes him rush over.

"Son of a bitch. Where the hell did you find that lighter?"

"I've lost my soul, Mary! Help me, my little Madonna!"

The nurse whooshes by and leaps to grab the lighter from the hands of the wacko. The wacko says nothing. He lets himself be laid back on the bed without any reaction, suddenly a limp, defenseless animal. "What am I supposed to do with you, Madonni'? Any more antics and I'm locking you in the bathroom, I swear."

My body wants to go back to sleep, but I fight back, try to resist, try to speak, yet I'm incapable.

The nurse turns to me, sweeps his hand over the smoldering side of my head. The air is heavy with the odor of burned chicken. He smiles condescendingly. "He didn't hurt you. Won't take more than two weeks for it to grow back."

With that, he's gone.

I manage to summon a small amount of lucidity, trying to understand, trying to fathom where I am. A large six-bed hospital room. Heat blending with the stink of disinfectant and sweat.

The man who yelled like a girl is looking around watchfully. One step at a time, he creeps closer. Impossible to escape. My incapacity to fight him off, even just scream, increases my terror. He smiles, steals closer to my face, my ear. "I'm a virgin," he whispers as if it were an irresistible invitation.

I'm scared. I wish I had my family here, my house, my room. I know why I'm here, I know what happened. The shame, the guilt. The memory of last night overwhelms me, it wants to melt into weeping. But it can't.

I fall back asleep, aching for tears that do not come.

Day 1
Tuesday

A hand on my shoulder is shaking me harder and harder.

"Mencarelli, come on, let's go."

It's the nurse, he's trying to wake me.

"Heeey, it's past eleven. You have to see the doctor in 15 minutes."

He grabs me by both shoulders and lifts me up.

"Good morning little prince, you certainly had a good rest. Not surprising, after what they shot you up with. Why don't you try telling me your name? What's your name?"

My mouth is parched. My head is pounding.

"Daniele. Daniele Mencarelli."

The nurse attempts a kind of smile. He's about 50, maybe a bit older. His face is pitted with deep pockmarks from acne back in the day.

"Good, Daniele. My name is Pino. Pino likes to make things clear right away. If you behave nice, I behave nice. If you act bad like a loony, I'll act worse than you. See? And believe me, us healthy people can be meaner than the loonies. Get that?"

Pino's face has hardened. I make an effort to answer despite my general numbness.

"I get it."

"One more thing. No wandering around. You either stay here or in the television room next door. Never, ever go to the rooms past the television room. They're not like you in there, they're bad people. You hear?"

"I hear."

"Good Daniele. Now, wake up properly. The doctor will call you soon. Here's some tea. Have a sip."

He hands me a tepid cup and leaves.

Repossessing my body makes me feel one by one a zillion pains scattered everywhere. Behind my back, around my neck. But the worst is the left hand. It's covered by a big bandage, caked with dried blood at the height of the knuckles. From the hand to my mind, the distance is short—against the walls, the furniture, the television screen until it explodes. Here are the marks. And finally, enormous as the sky, I see my father like a dead object on the floor, thanks to my performance.

A thicket of eyes. These are my roommates. The six beds are arranged in two rows. The three across from me are occupied. The young man in front of me is my age. While Pino was talking to me, I looked over at him from time to time. I am almost certain: ever since I started spying on him, he has not stopped staring at an undefined point above my head. As if he were looking through it. At something beyond that keeps him totally mesmerized. Even with everything going on around him he doesn't snap out of it.

To his left, beside the room's big window, there is a man of around sixty. Right off the bat, I notice his incredible similarity to the lead guitarist of Queen. I can't remember his name. The bed on the right is taken by the man with the girl's scream. Now he's looking at himself in a pocket mirror, applying lip gloss. In the meantime, he strikes poses, smiles at himself, seems to improvise a dialogue, a courtship.

I am in the middle bed of the other row. To my left is the lunatic who tried to set me on fire. He has calmed down, seems to even be sleeping.

The bed to the right is perfectly made, all neat, it must be free.

Every now and then, from other rooms, other worlds, come rants and moans that could shatter a rock.

*

Pino looks in.

"Hey Mencare'. Mancino is expecting you."

I struggle to get up. Remaining upright feels more compli-cated than usual. Pino takes me by the arm. We exit the room together, and enter the one right across the hall from us.

The doctor's office is small. Pino helps me sit down, then leaves.

The doctor is in front of me. What strikes me instantly is his bulk. It's extraordinary. I can tell from his arm, from the hand that is writing line after line with a pen pushed forcefully down on the white of the paper. At second glance, his head is enor-mous too, and his shoulders. I can't tell how tall he is, but he must be a giant.

"So, Mencarelli."

He speaks to me without lifting his eyes from the paper. Finally, he looks at me. His eyes are blue and very small; his nose is broad. His hair is half chestnut and the rest white. Even his face has something imposing, almost violent, about it. Had we been on friendlier terms, I would have asked if he played rugby, or used to play, because his overall appearance was def-initely that of a rugby player.

"Can you tell me today's date? Day, month, year."

I nod and start counting.

"Today is Tuesday 15 June 1994."

"Fourteen, Tuesday the 14th. Can you tell me what day, month and year you were born?"

"26 April 1974."

"So you're 20 years old. Do you know why you're here?"

In front of my eyes flicker the prickly, poisoned images of last night.

"Yes, because of last night."

The doctor observes me searchingly without changing his composure. The look in his eye plus his stature equals a man incapable of feeling emotions, at least this is the impression he gives.

"Do you have anything else to say? Do you want to tell me why it happened?"

"No, not for the moment." My refusal doesn't move him by a millimeter.

"As you wish. This afternoon, Doctor Cimaroli will be here. He's who took charge of you last night in the emergency room. He told me of your accomplishment. Congratulations. You came within a hair's breadth of killing your father. You must have a knack for measure."

I remain silent as he continues to study me. Every so often he takes notes on his very precious papers, which are most probably about me.

"Anyway. From today, you have been placed in involuntary psychiatric treatment. Do you know what that is? Doctor Cimaroli and his colleague at the emergency department opted for your committal. Here's how it works. We have given notice to the municipality where you live and the Tribunal of Velletri. This morning we received their permission via fax. So for seven days, you are obliged to remain here and receive care."

My chemical sluggishness vanishes in a flash. Hello anxiety and distress.

"What does that mean? Can't I go home?"

The doctor shakes his giant head no.

"From today Tuesday 14 June to next Monday 20, you'll be staying in our ward. Why, are you unhappy about that?"

The smile he displays leaves no doubt: my discomfort makes him cheerful.

"What if I behave well? If I have my parents come in, and you speak to them? I'm not a bad person. I've been in treatment for a few years now. I've seen some of your colleagues. I've never done harm to anyone."

"Well, your father's sudden collapse and the harm you've done to yourself mean that from now on, we will be deciding if you are a danger or not. We'll assess what's wrong with you and what isn't wrong. What are the names of my colleagues who treated you?"

"I can't remember them all. Sanfilippo, Lorefice, Castro and maybe a few others."

"Your parents must have spent a pretty penny sending you to all those expensive doctors. We'll have the chance to look into all this. Our meeting now is just to tell you about the involuntary commitment. I am Doctor Mancino. This afternoon we'll be seeing Doctor Cimaroli together. You can go back to your room. God damn the heat in this hospital!"

The final imprecation, spoken to himself, comes out half in dialect. Definitely from the South, but I couldn't say where.

From the doctor's office to my room, it must be about ten steps. I walk slowly. The faces of my father, mother, brother and sister accompany me in silence. Ever since I was born, I have done nothing but create havoc, one over-the-top incident after another. Always following my gut feeling, for better or for worse. I am unable to live in another way, I cannot escape this ferocity: if there is a peak I must reach it; if there is an abyss I must touch it.

From my bed, I see Doctor Mancino stride by. With his erect posture and brisk pace, he looks like a true giant.

I try to catch his eye, but he doesn't want to know about it. He emanates resentment, if not contempt. His face remains impressed on my mind: how can you detest so openly the very person you are supposed to heal? Over the past two years, my Via Crucis of psychiatrists and pathologies has made me used to detachment and indifference, but such a clear declaration of disdain coming from a doctor is something I have not yet experienced.

"Ciao."

Without me noticing, the man with the girl's scream has appeared at my side.

"Mancino's some tough cookie, eh? But he's not the worst in here, believe me. My name's Gianluca." He offers me a nail-painted hand.

"Daniele," I say, shaking it.

"You involuntary commitment like me?"

I nod.

"Me too, since yesterday. What'd you do?"

Gianluca must be in his forties with thinning hair. Its multiple colors range from ash to chemically burned to bright red. He has engineered a long comb-over to mask a bald patch. His pinched lips are glossy and smiling. I do not answer his question, but he is not intimidated.

"I get it. Well I did something stupid. I brought a friend home and that vicious old hag of my mother started tripping out. Believe me, really tripping so bad I had to smack her. But I'm a good person, good as gold in every way." And he produces another smile that aims to be provocative, while I think of the words I just wasted on Mancino. Who knows how often his patients try to convince him of their goodness.

"Now let Gianluca give you the lay of the land in this room. So, in the bed next to the window is Mario. He was an elementary school teacher before he got crazy. He's a good egg, too."

Hearing his name, Mario turns toward us, smiles, and goes back to staring at the tree right outside the window. Gianluca comes closer to me.

"He says there's a birdie in the tree, but nobody has ever seen it. Anyhow, let me continue. In the bed next to Mario there's Alessandro. He's catatonic. This afternoon his father's coming, and he'll tell you all about it, like he does with everyone. The other bed is mine. On this side there's Madonnina, the one who was setting you on fire. They call him Madonnina because no one knows anything about him. He doesn't talk, except with the Holy Mary from time to time. All of them are hospitalized. Only you and I are involuntary. We've got a lot in common." When he finishes, he lands a kiss on my cheek and bursts into laughter that's hard, forced.

"Isn't life just great!" he shouts one centimeter from my face.

I remain silent, my eyes scooting from bed to bed, from one insanity to the next. Slowly, the tears I was yearning for, waiting for, well up.

"Hey gentlemen, it's lunch-time." Pino looks in from the door. I call him over, bawling uncontrollably.

"I want to go home. Please." I grip his arm. He pries it free delicately.

"Don't do this. A week will be over in no time. You'll see, you'll feel better."

He raises his voice, "Today! Broth or soup, boiled potatoes or peas, chicken breast or pork chop. Let's go!"

Pino starts serving lunch. The mere sight of the array of dishes makes what little hunger I had disappear entirely. But Gianluca and Madonnina eat voraciously. Alessandro the catatonic is still fixated on the point half a meter above my head. Nothing in our realm interests him, not even food.

"Are you eating that baked apple?" Mario has appeared at my side. His white curly hair sits like a tall unruly hedge on top of his head.

Of the different courses being served, the only one that attracted my attention ever so slightly was precisely the baked apple, out of sheer emotional attachment. My mother raised me on them. Baked apples were the unfailing side dish of every flu I came down with, and any other bug, for that matter.

"No, you have it. No worries," I reply. I had seen great

smiles before, many of them, marvelous ones, but this one seemed to outdo them all. It was great for the amount of unguarded gratitude you could imagine inside it.

"Mario only eats baked apples. We give him all of ours," Gianluca hastens to explain, taking up his role of self-proclaimed expert guide to the ward.

"Thank you," Mario says, looking into my eyes with liquid eyes.

My curiosity becomes unbearable. It surpasses my desire to flee. I call Pino over, beckoning him with my head.

"Don't think I'm out of my mind. I know this is the nuthouse. But do you know the band Queen? Freddie Mercury?"

Pino nods yes, "I know, he's identical to the guitarist Brian May, just that Mario is older and crazier."

"I couldn't remember his name. Thanks."

At two in the afternoon I see Pino in plain clothes exit the building with swift strides. He does not reciprocate my handwave. In his place, another nurse appears, a younger and slimmer one.

The heat is the big room is stifling. Only Gianluca and I appear to be suffering from it. Madonnina and Alessandro seem to not notice. Mario has even donned a heavy, rumpled dressing gown on top of his pajamas, which are also heavy, for winter use.

I grab a 200-lire coin from the pair of pants thrown into my locker. There's a payphone at the ward's entrance, next to the door they keep barred.

"Danie'?"

I always thought my mother had a supernatural power, especially with us children, a gift that allows her to understand things quicker and better, beyond all possible words, beyond all artfully construed lies. She knew it was me on the other end of the line. The absolute certainty of her love that could break the laws of physics, took away what little strength I had mustered.

"Yes, it's me."

"How are you?"

She had transmitted a bit of her gift to us by blood, or maybe no gift was needed to notice all her worry.

"Fine now. They're keeping me here for a week, did you know?"

"The doctor told us last night, and we agreed. You don't realize it, but you sort of went insane. How do you feel now?"

My hand runs over the Madonnina-seared part of my scalp. My fingers caress the naked skin. Fortunately only the hair burned.

"I'm fine, except that they're all lunatics in here, but I mean real lunatics."

My mother stops speaking, and then takes up the conversation once again. I understand the reason for her silence. Her voice is trembling, but she masters it.

"We've been going from doctor to doctor for two years and none of them understands a thing. Maybe in there, they'll find out what's bothering you. Because a 20-year-old is supposed to be happy, but you're running on unhappiness. We can't figure out how to get it off your back."

The self-control she had imposed crumbles like dry dirt. "I just want to see you happy," is all she succeeds in saying before the sobbing starts.

"But I'm not unhappy. This isn't about unhappiness. I feel like I'm the only one who understands that we're all tightrope walkers. From one moment to the next, we stop breathing and they slip us into a coffin, like nothing happened. Time seems like an insult to you, to Papa, and it makes me furious. But sometimes I could make light bulbs glow with all the happiness I have inside. In fact, no one knows what happiness means like I do."

My mother retrieves her faculty of speech. Her breathing sounds more natural, too.

"This afternoon your brother will be coming there to bring you some fresh clothes. I got you some cookies and juice. Do you need anything else?"

I'd like to tell my mother what I really need. It's always the same thing, ever since I screeched my first cry to the world. For a long time, it was not easy to say what I wanted. I tried to explain by complicated concepts, and spent these first twenty years of my life studying the best words to describe it. I used many words, too many, and then I understood that I needed to proceed in the opposite direction. So, day by day, I began subtracting one, the least necessary one, a superfluous one. Little by little I shortened and pruned them until I only had one word left. One word to say what I really want, this thing I've been carrying since birth, before birth. It follows me like a shadow, always lying by my side.

Salvation. I do not mention this word to anyone but myself. But this is the word, and its meaning is bigger than death.

Salvation. For me. For my mother at the other end of the telephone. For all children and all mothers. And fathers. And all sisters and brothers of all past and future times. My illness is called salvation. So now what? Who can I tell it to?

Perhaps this thing I call salvation is but one of the many names of the illness. Perhaps it doesn't exist, and me wishing for it is just a symptom in need of a cure. What terrorizes me is not the idea that I'm ill, which is something I am getting used to, but the doubt that everything is just a coincidence of the cosmos, the human being as a regurgitation of life, by mistake.

"No Mamma, I don't need anything else. Make sure you stop worrying and stay calm, all right?"

"I'll be calm when you're back home."

"I've lost my soul, Mary! Help me, my little Madonna!"

Madonnina is awake now, sitting on his bed, hands open in front of his eyes. He seems to study them, first the backs, then the palms. He looks amazed at his ability to control them. I arrive at my bed and lie down. He's about one meter from me. I can't guess how old he is, maybe around thirty. His cheeks are hollow, his beard unkempt, his remote eyes sunken deep. His threadbare pajamas hang open, showing a few sparse hairs on his chest. Above all, he's so emaciated you could count his bones. But it's not his exhausted appearance that makes my heart bleed, that makes me close my eyes for an instant, overcome by compassion. His appearance is a sad consequence, the melted wax of a candle. What makes me cry is the black coal that consumes his eyes. They smolder with agony so deep it takes my breath away. What illness can place such an enormous weight on a man's shoulders? The weight bearing down on Madonnina's poor body is beastly, inhuman. I force myself to not look at him, and I'm ashamed of this. Just for a second, my mind flashes with the thought that the beast of anguish that enslaves him might jump on me and take me, too.

My eyes wander over the room. Besides Madonnina, there's only my neighbor across the way, Alessandro, steadily staring above my head. I decide to stretch my legs and look for a human being still able to speak. From the room next door comes the voice of Marta Flavi. Here comes Mario from the bathroom. He smiles as he slips by slowly to reach the window.

Perusing the hallway, I have the chance to familiarize myself with the layout of the ward. Our room, the doctor's office across the way, another few closed doors, a medical dispensary and the public toilets form a kind of first group of facilities with the television room. Right after, a barred door with opaque glass like the main access door probably leads to the other round, where the bad people are. That's what I figure.

I see Gianluca and the nurse who has replaced Pino

engrossed in front of the TV. As soon as the nurse sees me, he gets up and walks over. "Ciao," he says.

I respond with a nod. He's thirty max, awkward and timid.

"My name's Lorenzo. Let me be clear right away. Don't break my balls, and I won't break yours. Understood?"

Nurse Lorenzo has replicated Pino's warning in a somewhat clumsier manner and with less capacity to instill respect. Thanks to him, I understand the real meaning of those words. They attack you first, in order to hide their fear of being attacked.

I can tell Lorenzo is afraid. There's no fiber of his body that doesn't signal this. It can't be easy spending every day in the company of a drove of crack-brains.

"Don't worry, really, I'm very peaceful. My name's Daniele." But my attempt to reassure him does not have much effect.

"Cimaroli's coming for you shortly. As soon as he's ready, I'll call you," says Lorenzo and leaves the room.

Marta Flavi is on the television interviewing a forty-year-old man, the zillionth broken heart looking for new love.

"Well, physically he's a mess. He might be a nice guy. But not all of us can be good-looking like Daniele, for instance," Gianluca gets back on track, having noticed my presence. He bats his eyes, smiles, then he gets all lascivious. I react.

"Gianlu', I'm just going to say this once and for all. I like girls. Is that clear? If you want, we can be friends, that's fine, but don't keep acting like you're going to jump my bones all the time, because you're getting on my nerves. Got that?"

He responds by leaning his face close into mine, his eyes feverish with desire. "You don't know what you're missing, especially my mouth."

I remain immobile, do nothing to hide how much he irks me.

Gianluca tries to continue his seduction spiel, but the wind has gone out of his sail. "So what the hell. Sure, friends. Whenever I'm in an up, all I can think of is sex. I wish I could get a grip, but I have all this energy, I'm continuously horny, I'm hungry for it all the time."

I think of his words, trying not to react, but fail.

"Can I ask you something? I'm curious to know what an up is."

Gianluca leans in again.

"I am severely bipolar, nothing I can do about it. The up phase is when I feel good, too good. Even the doctors tell me that all this euphoria is a symptom. I feel good, but it's really the disorder making me feel that way. Then there's the down phase, when I feel terribly bad. It's awful. Last time, I lost so much weight I was down to forty-seven kilos. When I'm up, I only think of sex. When I'm down, my only thought is death." Gianluca tries to smile, but cannot.

"Anyways, I know I'll end up stuck in the down phase sooner or later." An ominous shadow clouds his eyes, as if he were seeing his end. For a moment, the screaming girl from this morning flashes over his face. She has surrendered to the fear, cowers under a few strands of bleached hair, whitened stubble on her cheeks.

I look at him and his entire being seems to ask for help.

"Don't talk nonsense. You're strong. I'll tell you what we'll do. I'll call Marta Flavi and ask her to introduce you to the ugly duckling sitting next to her."

Gianluca drinks my words and he beams again. "Good idea. You might come visit us one night."

"Sure, I could bring you pastries."

"Don't get me started on pastries. Besides sex, that's another thing I can't resist."

Lorenzo pokes his head around the glass door.

"Mencarelli, to the doctor's office."

I rise as Gianluca returns to Marta Flavi.

"Say hello to the doctors," he says.

In the office, I find Doctor Mancino alongside another whitecoat—fiftyish, puffy face, round eyeglasses. The latter stoke my memory.

As soon as I'm within arm's reach, he offers his hand.

"Do you remember me?"

I nod.

"I'm Doctor Cimaroli. I was called into the emergency room last night for a consultation. Let's say you were a bit worked up."

"Unfortunately, yes," I acquiesce.

"I tried to ask you what had angered you so much, but you didn't want to answer. In the end, we had to sedate you twice. I've rarely seen a person so agitated. We needed four people to hold you down. Do you feel like talking about it now?"

My desire to talk is motivated by more than just the hope of getting the involuntary commitment lifted. I also feel the need to let out whatever it was that last night's anger was not able to assuage.

"As soon as I finished high school I enrolled in the university to study law. At the same time, I started working as a salesman of air-conditioning units. That's where it all began, at work."

Cimaroli listens attentively to my story. Mancino, on the other hand, shows by his posture and facial expression that he's bored out of his head.

"The other day, my company gave me the name of some customers in Cisterna di Latina. My region is further north—from Valmontone to Arsoli, more or less—but they decided I had to go there. It was an elderly couple. I go in, measure the place to calculate how big the unit needs to be. They're happy, everything's normal. Then, their son comes out of one of the rooms. I know this sounds like a small detail. He was about thirty-five. He sits down close to me, smiles and starts caressing my cheek like a child would do. The father starts telling me,

'You'd never know it, but he's an engineer, a nuclear engineer. He used to work in Poland. Had a car accident in the snow. Was in a coma for almost one year. Now he's like this.'"

My words bring me back to that apartment. I'm facing the old parents, the son who reverted to childhood. My suffering bubbles up all over again.

"What then?" asks Cimaroli. His kind eyes are looking at me.

"It wasn't the father's story as much as the caresses. At a certain point, it felt like the whole thing was an act, so I got up, told them that the unit wouldn't be powerful enough to cool and heat the entire house, and said that they'd be spending a truck-load of money on electricity. Finally, I fled. I went back to the road, dumped my briefcase in a garbage pail, and left. But I couldn't stop thinking of that guy. I started getting angry. Why does no one realize that we're like feathers in the wind? Just a little breeze blows us away. How is it that you raise a son, you take the bread from your own mouth to send him to school, and he comes back to you as a four-year-old? Why is that? What the hell is this all for? I arrived in Albano, wanting to end it all somehow. I bumped into a friend who sells cocaine. I bought three grams with all the money I had, thinking it would help me, you know, end the story."

With all the heat and the words streaming out in desperation, I realize I'm soaking wet. Cimaroli notices, jumps up, exits the door and comes back with a half-liter bottle of water. He hands it to me, and I drain half of it with one gulp.

"Then what happened?"

"I went home. My parents were over at my sister's in-laws for dinner. I sniffed the three grams in two lines, but wasn't able to go through with it, so I emptied my father's bottle of whisky. Finally, the rage came out, but it wasn't enough for what I wanted to do, so I destroyed the house. At eleven my father came home. As soon as he saw me, he fainted. It was a nervous breakdown, luckily. Then I went to the emergency room."

"Well thank God your rage wasn't sufficient. At least now you're here and you can let us help you, no?"

"Yes, but . . ."

"Speak freely."

"What cure can exist for how life is? I mean, it's all meaningless, and when you talk about meaning, people look at you oddly. But is it wrong to look for meaning? Why do I need to have a meaning? If you don't have it, how do you explain it all, how do you explain death? How can you deal with the death of someone you love? If it's all senseless, I can't accept it, so I want to die."

"Do they talk about religion at home? Is your mother very religious?"

This time it was Mancino interrogating. Something in my story must have reached him.

"They never go to church. My father's a socialist. My mother's a communist. She carries photos of Enrico Berlinguer and Pope John XXIII in her wallet. There's never any talk of religion except for at christenings, weddings and funerals. What does that have to do with anything?"

"The subjects of sense and meaning are religious references, and God is a cultural factor."

"What do you mean, cultural?"

"Let's say it's like the alphabet. Someone has to teach it to you."

I can't tell if the confusion I experience at that moment is visible from the outside.

"To understand it better, what is the opposite of cultural? For instance, is death cultural?" I ask.

"Death exists. It's a fact. Then humans and their civilizations found different ways to explain it and give it a meaning that it otherwise would not have."

"So if I look at my mother, or my father, and feel that the love I have for them is timeless, has no expiration date, is this because they taught me so? Because otherwise, what would love be without this teaching?"

Mancino sighs loudly, stares at me as if I were a flea.

"This is intellectualism. Some people function in a different way, often for quite simple chemical reasons. Just to give you an example, have you ever heard of selective serotonin reuptake inhibitors?" Mancino asks me.

"No," I reply.

"Serotonin is a neurotransmitter. You might have a deficit of this neurotransmitter."

Cimaroli places his hand on his colleague's shoulder and says, "We might want to ask him about the treatment he has had, just so we know."

Mancino nods listlessly.

"Can you tell us who is in charge of your treatment and what pharmaceuticals they've prescribed and why?" asks Cimaroli.

"I already told your colleague the names of the doctors. I remember Lorefice, Sanfilippo and Castro. There was a lot of medicine. I won't be able to remember it all." I stop to put order in my memories and the names.

"So, first of all there was Anafranil, an antidepressant. Other than making me impotent, it did nothing for me. Then there was Carbolithium, and that didn't help me either, but it did make my skin and hair oily. Then Mutabon, Tegretol, Depakin, and all the benzodiazepines for insomnia. There were probably others, but I can only remember these ones for now."

"These are for very diverse disorders," Cimaroli observes.

"Each doctor made their own evaluation. I can't say much about that, because I always told the same story, more or less."

Mancino stretches. For him, the visit has come to an end.

"Good. Naturally, we will issue a diagnosis at the end of the treatment."

I look into the eyes of both doctors. I try to come across as serious and calm as possible.

"I swear I have learned my lesson. Please send me home."

Mancino does not deign my request with a reply. I can tell Cimaroli feels sorry for me.

"Believe me, you need this period of observation time. Don't worry, this is a small ward. I want to ask you one last thing. Do you use cocaine often? Other drugs?"

"During the week, I smoke hashish. Sometimes weed. Friday and Saturday nights I take stronger stuff, usually ecstasy, or when I can't find the pills, cocaine. Always with friends."

"For someone with your nervous system, taking one pill is like taking a hundred. I don't want to preach, but it's true. Are you still studying law?"

"No, I quit a few months ago."

"Do you have any projects? Hobbies? Something you'd enjoy doing?"

I'm embarrassed to say it, but in the end I do: "I've been writing poetry since the end of middle school."

Cimaroli smiles and smacks me on the back.

"Bravo. If you want, you can read something to me next time."

My embarrassment reaches a peak.

"Except for my mother and an ex-girlfriend, I've never read it to anyone."

Mancino rises and takes leave of Cimaroli with a nod of his head. He ignores me. One thing he'd said sticks in my mind. If I don't get if off my chest now, it's going to obsess me all night long, I'm sure.

"Doctor Mancino." He turns toward me with absolute annoyance.

"Before, you said that my problem might be simply chemical. It would be great if it were just a question of chemicals, if all we needed to do is add some or take some away. I'd be the happiest guy in the world. But for now, everything I've tried hasn't changed a thing."

He smiles as if looking at a dog trying to perform a trick it will never be able to learn, as if seeing an animal that does not know its own limits.

"We just need to find the right drug," he says.

I return to my room. A middle-aged, pint-sized man follows me in. I'm short, but he's much shorter, probably 1 meter 60 tall, and that's being kind.

From his tanned face it's easy to guess he works outdoors. He goes to sit down next to Alessandro. He takes from a shopping bag a pack of yoghurt and a bottle of water. Every now and then he glances over at my spot, where I have flopped down sweaty after my exhausting conversation with the doctors.

"Did you get here this morning?" he asks, delicately opening one of the two containers of yoghurt.

"Last night."

"What's wrong?"

"Dunno. They don't know either. They said they'll tell me at the end of my stay."

"You seem normal, perfectly fine."

In the meantime he had begun feeding his son, trying to feed him, that is. He reminds me of my aunt trying to make my two-year-old cousin eat while he purses his lips.

"You see him? He seems normal too, right? Always been normal. When he finished middle school, he came to work with me. I've been a mason for forty years. He was my assistant. It takes time to learn the trade, but he was quite quick. Then one day." He stops to wipe the corners of his son's mouth. Of all the yoghurt only a minimal amount reaches its destination. The rest drips down his face.

"See him? Stubborn. He only eats for me. As I was saying, one day a few months ago, we were renovating an apartment in

Castello. We had no more plaster and I say to him, 'Alessa', I'm going to the supply store.' I thought I'd give him a reward, so I say, 'Why don't you pull up the partition wall?' He was all proud because it was the first time I gave him a big job to do. I leave, and when I come back, he's like this, like you see him now. He had started pulling up the partition, but he must have not measured it properly. It was crooked, all out of whack. How can you get like this just from a partition?"

The father rests the yoghurt on the nightstand, extracts a carefully folded handkerchief from the pocket of his jacket, and dries his eyes.

"You know, I'm alone. His mother ran away with a Pole many years ago. I wouldn't even know where to look for her."

From the inside pocket of the same jacket he takes a small comb. He slides it out of its soft case. It's identical to the one my father keeps in the glove compartment of the car.

He starts combing his son's hair carefully, beginning with the sides. A patch at the back of his neck gives him a particularly hard time. Alessandro does not unhitch his eyes from the absolute void, still half a meter above my head. It takes some time and a bit of perseverance but, finally, the rebellious lock of hair is smoothed.

What illness makes me ask for salvation?

What upbringing makes me beg for mercy?

Make me only have a chemical imbalance. Give me all the pharmaceuticals in the world, but close my eyes and heart, for I cannot bear to suffer like this for all that I see and hear.

Like an astronaut exploring an alien planet, my brother's face appears at the door. He peeks in, fearing to enter. I gesture for him to stay there and at the same time I get up off the bed. I go over.

"Best we keep out in the hallway."

My brother is incredulous. He takes in every detail of this Martian land, its howls, deranged faces, and walls peeling under the madness. Then he notices the bald swath on the side of my head.

"What the hell did you do to your hair?"

"Nothing. My roommate did it, but it's over now."

"Holy shit, look at where you ended up."

"How many changes of clothes did you bring me?"

He hands me a big bag.

"Mamma gave you three pairs of underwear and three T-shirts. She said she'd come by tomorrow."

His bewilderment and dread give me absolute determination.

"No. Look at this place. I don't want Mamma here, not for any reason."

"Yeah, best not to have her come."

"Now you leave, too."

My brother doesn't wait for me to say it again. He looks at me one last time, hugs me fleetingly, almost ashamed.

Supper is served at six-thirty. It's a repeat of the lunch ritual. Gianluca wolfs it all down. Madonnina eats too, but slower. Mario's tray has four plastic plates, each with a baked apple on it. He organizes them with millimetric, chilling precision. I notice, now, that everything around his bed is neat as a pin, folded better than in the army. The orderliness clashes with his flannel pajamas, worn and creased. How he can stand wearing them in this heat only the mental disorder knows. At least he has taken off the heavy robe for dinner. Now and again he looks out the window toward the tree and its branches, smiles in that direction at a specific point. Then he takes up fork and knife with the bearing of a disgraced prince, and starts on the first baked apple.

I am eating, too. Chocolate cookies, one of the packs my brother brought me. I didn't even look at the hospital food.

The sun is still high. Who knows what my friends are doing. Given the hour, I bet they're sprawled out in the Villa Doria park, passing around a joint. This week the World Cup soccer championship starts. We were organizing an evening together to watch the national team play. They mustn't know anything about my involuntary commitment, they wouldn't understand. I'll invent something. A week of unexpected work. A refresher course away from home.

I have to tell my employer that I quit. I hope they don't ask me to give back the catalogues and the note pads for orders. They're in my briefcase inside a dumpster in the middle of nowhere on the outskirts of Cisterna di Latina.

"What's up?"

In the throes of good humor, Gianluca chirps the question around to everybody. I can't say what his head is telling him, but it seems like he doesn't feel he's in the room of a psychiatric ward. Rather he's in a hotel suite with his buddies, ready to spend the evening having fun in a thousand ways, a place like you might find, say, on the Adriatic Riviera.

No one answers.

Mario is meticulously cleaning his food tray, folding the paper napkin to perfection before he drops it in the trash.

Madonnina has finished his meal, and now lies in a fetal position, ready to surrender to sweet oblivion.

Each minute lasts for ages. One century passes before the sun sets. It's after nine. I bide my time by reading a newspaper my mother put in with the other stuff. Everything is about the national soccer team. I don't like the coach Arrigo Sacchi, but you can't say he's not brilliant. Roberto Baggio is the real prince of the nation; how could you not agree. Yet I wouldn't underestimate Beppe Signori, who plays for Lazio, which is unforgivable, but he's a raptor. Not many others attack the goal like he does. The Italian team begins its group stage against Ireland on Saturday, and I'll be locked up inside here. The summers when there's the World Cup are the best ones.

Immense nostalgia tells me the story of life on the outside as if it were a marvelous island, but I am shipwrecked. Apart from that, I succeed at little else.

"Lights out, gentlemen."

A fiftyish woman tells us it's time to sleep. Everything here is commanded. Politely, but still commanded. Her eyes rest on me.

"You must be the new vacationer."

"So it would seem," I reply.

"I'm Rossana. I do the night shift."

Unlike her male colleagues, she doesn't feel threatened and so doesn't need to threaten.

She turns off the light.

The first sleepless night I can remember was 6 January 1985. The next day, we were supposed to go back to school after the Christmas vacation, but during the night, the prayers of all the students from Rome and its provinces were fulfilled. So much snow. A gift from heaven. I was glued to the window the whole time, first to watch it fall, then to see it turn into a shimmering carpet from under which nothing could escape. That was the only night I was happy to not sleep. After that, thousands of others followed, nights I chased sleep, courted her like the hottest girl. The worst nights are the ones after ecstasy. You lie down out of habit, knowing perfectly well that sleep will not come. Your jaw tenses, your wide eyes stare at the ceiling, your heart vibrates in your ribcage.

But here, now, it's not my insomnia preventing me from dozing off.

It's not any of the drugs in the world, either.

Here, now, not even those who sleep like blessed angels would be able to sleep.

Like wolves and other nocturnal beasts stirred up by the darkness, now the wailing, the voices, the deliriums commence.

In this room, too.

Mario is the most tormented one. He weeps, speaks of one Angelica, cries out.

The fear suddenly makes me feel cold. I cover myself with the sheet even though I'm sweating from the heat. This morning, the person who now sleeps beside me tried to set me on fire. Across from me is a guy who never stops staring half a meter above my head. Then there are two more crazies.

I want to escape.

What would the legal consequences be for someone who escapes from involuntary commitment?

Where to escape from? Except for the window, every entrance is locked.

I ring the bell.

I get up, deciding not to wait for nurse Rossana. I find her in the hall walking toward me.

"Could you give me something to make me sleep? The shouting is keeping me awake. Please."

Rossana doesn't even answer. She turns on her clogs and heads back to the medical dispensary.

"I beg you. They're driving me crazy. Please."

She stops. Her makeup-less face is weighted down by Father Time.

"I'm sorry, but without the doctor's permission I cannot give you anything."

"Can't you go get permission?"

"Not at this hour. If they agree, it'll be tomorrow morning at the earliest."

"Then I'm getting out of here."

I wasn't talking to her, but to myself.

Rossana looks at me, vaguely resentful.

"Stay here."

She quickly strides over to the dispensary, and returns.

"Here. I'll tell the doctor tomorrow morning."

The pill is microscopic, greenish. It looks like a miniature Zigulì candy.

"What's this? I've never seen one."

"Phenergan. It's an antihistamine, but we give them for sleeping. Now get in there and go to bed."

I remain in the corridor with the pill in my hand, then swallow it without water.

Silence reigns in the room. No sooner have I taken note of this than Mario starts up wailing again.

The others seem to be asleep.

For now, the pill does not work. I hope Rossana hasn't fobbed me with one of her grandchildren's candies just to appease me.

I open my eyes and there's light.

Nurse Rossana's little candy, Phenergan or whatever it's called, is a marvel of a substance. Unlike benzodiazepines, which give you a groggy, sluggish wake-up, from this thing you awake completely lucid. On the downside, you don't feel like you've had much rest. All in all, it's a drug that merits consideration.

One of the psychiatrists I went to, I think it was Sanfilippo, told me at the end of a session that I have a tendency toward addiction, an attraction to dependency-forming substances. Perhaps out of fear, I initially convinced myself he was wrong. However, his evaluation turned out to be one of the few accurate ones I have received regarding my mental health. If the pill at hand is able to relieve me of myself for a little while, if it succeeds in placating the ballistic engine racing in my chest, then it's welcome.

Yet few drugs succeed in calming me down, least of all the so-called soft drugs. Hashish produces the exact opposite effect. It relaxes my body, but excites my mind, making it race at high speed, so quick that it makes me forget each thought as soon as it's formed. Plus it increases my anxiety. I never tell anyone, but it does do that.

Weed, depending on the strain, is less aggressive, but I have known earth-moving kinds. The most potent is the one my friend Damiano grows on his balcony. He dries it upside down behind the closet in his garage. One evening we went out with

his friend from military service, a guy from Genoa, really fun. He was in the habit of sniffing heroine with his buddies on Saturday nights. We were in the car passing a joint, headed for Rome. We had to pull over. We were unable to keep our eyes open, and we're used to substances. One joint, just one, knocked out four young lads. We woke up the next morning still dazed. Damiano's military friend told us he had never been floored like that, not even by a shot of heroin.

The other drugs, the chemical ones, do not placate me, but they do make the agitation inhabiting me more sociable. They turn it into an amusing game, at least when I'm high. But the down is devastating; it gets worse with every extra pill. Along with insomnia, it builds an invincible monster. Each time, Saturday after Saturday, the high is shorter, so you ratchet up the swallowing of pills, from one to two, then three, then ten. A few friends even take fifteen on a Saturday night. In the end, they look grotesque with their jaws unhinged from the rest of their sunken face, like the living dead. But the first ecstasy pills were like going back to when I was six on Christmas morning, finding under the tree the gift I had dreamed of for months on end. It was the same bliss, the same boundless joy as far as the eye can see, and the energy to make you dance all night long. But only at the start. One Saturday at a time, the enchantment turns into a hex. The state of grace becomes more and more elusive. You have to chase it from club to club, and feed it pills as you go.

The joy does not return. In its place arrive characters who were not invited to the party, car accidents, arrests, brain after brain consumed by amusement.

In any case, out of intellectual honesty, I must ascribe to Doctor Sanfilippo one of the few correct conclusions concerning the magma coursing through my veins.

On my nightstand I find a cup of tea, or something that

aspires to be tea, still steaming. Next to it lie an individually wrapped packet of rusks and a portion-pack of cherry jam.

My roommates have already had breakfast. Gianluca and Madonnina are not around. My neighbor across the way is still half a meter above my head, hypnotized. What if Alessandro's catatonic state were precisely that, hypnosis? The father said that when his son turned blank, he was alone, raising a partition wall, but maybe some entity made him this way. I mean not a person, but an alien, a demon or something like that. Who knows?

I regret my idea right away. It's the result of all the horror movies I watch on Italia Uno. In the end anyway, what does it matter—disorder or demon, Alessandro is like an insect crystallized in invisible amber, and for the moment no one is having success in freeing him.

Madonnina is still sleeping, a mere slip of a human being, all folded up with his head in between his arms.

"Psst."

It's Mario, he wants my attention. He motions me over. I go. Except for yesterday's baked-apple request, there has not been any contact between us.

When I get to his side, he takes my shoulders and turns me toward the evergreen crown of the tree, then bends me a bit to one side.

"Look between the two biggest branches. Can you see it?"

I follow his instructions, but see nothing.

"So? Do you see it?"

I don't know what to do. Go along with him or not? Then, between the fronds, camouflaged like only animals are capable of, I make out a small nest. Throning it is a tiny bird, very pretty, moving its head with little jerks. For eyes it has two shiny black beads.

"I see it!" I turn to Mario, smile at him, grateful for the beauty he has invited me to share. He reciprocates, showing a face full of pure happiness. I think of bad-mouth Gianluca. As

soon as I see him I'm going to tell him that Mario's birdie is not the usual gibble-gabble you hear so much of around here.

"Now you're not going to believe me, but once I saw one of them come back to life. I'm sure it was dead, but then it was resuscitated. It started moving and then flew away. I'm sure you don't believe me, but if you had seen it you wouldn't have the shadow of a doubt."

I don't know what to say. Then he relieves me of my embarrassment.

"I've been here for a couple of weeks. My name is Mario, I know you know that."

"Yes, yesterday morning Gianluca gave me a tour of the room. My name is Daniele."

"I know. Did you also know I used to be a teacher?"

I nod.

"How come you're in here? It's a stupid question, but curiosity loves certainty, even when it doesn't exist. Young and old love it."

"I don't know how to answer. I've been going from doctor to doctor for a few years now. They've been diagnosing almost all existing pathologies."

"The usual ones?" Mario asks.

"What do you mean?"

"I mean neuroses, the ones based on anxiety, phobia, depression—they're the most in vogue."

"Yes, that's more or less the case," I say.

I'm about to tell him how incredibly much he resembles Brian May from Queen, but in the end I'm too shy.

Doctor Cimaroli arrives at the doorway.

"Good morning, gentlemen," and he leaves.

"The shaman has arrived," says Mario, eyeing the door. His name for Cimaroli makes me smile.

"Why shaman?" I ask.

"Because science understands a certain amount of what

goes on from the feet to the neck, but up here?" He points to his head. "Nothing yet. We're still in the shaman era. The rites and magic formulas have changed, herbs have become pills, but truthfully, medicine is groping in the dark. We might wake up tomorrow and hear that they're no longer sure about the disease they labeled us with, that what triggers this or that pathology is not what they always thought it was."

I don't wish to hurt his feelings, but his view seems exaggerated to me. He notices.

"It's okay if you don't believe me, but I assure you that's how it is. Tomorrow, the news will arrive from Boston or Tokyo or somewhere else that a learned wizard has made a new study of a specific part of the brain and that his study affirms with certainty that this mental disorder is not what the scientific community has always thought. They'll say, 'Ladies and gentlemen, this here is the true nature of the disorder.' But in reality, it's just the latest hypothesis. Everything changes. But it's fine if you don't believe me. You're still young, and if you're lucky you'll find a doctor who's on the ball, someone who wishes to understand their patients' suffering at all costs. I did meet one, but he flew to heaven prematurely."

Mario speaks Italian without a lilt. It's clean and enunciated the way it should be. Plus, I don't know if he does it on purpose, but he seems to caress his interlocutor with his eyes every time he looks at them. It's a gift, a sweetness that you'd expect in an entirely different place, not in this nuthouse.

"If I may ask, how is it that you're in here?"

Mario stops me.

"Between crackpots, no need for such formality."

"So what are you doing here?" I rephrase.

Mario returns to his bird of flesh and bones. His curls quiver in the thin breeze entering the window. The air is already boiling hot.

"Things persecute me. I'm unable to send them away. There is no escape possible. I drown in my own mind."

Mario's eyes, those champions of tenderness, are swimming in the abyss. He turns toward his worn dressing gown and puts it on. Wherever he is now, it's freezing.

"Gentlemen, a new guest!"

It's Pino. He accompanies his announcement with a theatrical flourish, stopping at the bed next to mine.

"Allow me to introduce Giorgio! His fourth involuntary commitment of the year! An applause, please."

Pino would like to take a bow, but his paunch is in the way and this puts an end to his desire for fun and games.

The new tenant appears at the door. He's a hulking lump of a man, about thirty years old, at least 1 meter 90 tall. An undershirt covers his enormous chest. His arms are twice mine. He carries a shopping bag, nothing else. He frowns in our direction, heads for the empty bed next to mine and sits down. The springs of the skimpy mattress groan.

"Mario, Mancino's expecting you. Let's go."

"See you later," Mario takes leave with a smile. I smile back.

In the big room, it's only me and the new guy.

"Ciao," I attempt to introduce myself, but the big beast Giorgio is uninterested.

Without him noticing me, I spy on him. He has lain down. His face is covered by a thick rug of shapeless hair. Underneath it, his massive features show through. His nose is like a boxer's, crushed. His jaw-line is pronounced, and his lips are, too.

"Ciao," he answers as he rises from the bed with unexpected litheness for his mass. Finally he looks over at me. He goes toward the door, looks out to the right and to the left, then shuts the double doors. I don't understand the latter action. Furtively, he turns to me.

"Com'ere."

It was a little after eleven in the morning. It must have already been thirty degrees Celsius, but hot and cold do not depend only on the temperature—poor Mario knows something about that. A sequence of thoughts rushes through my mind.

What do I do?

Ask for help? Who the hell would come help me? Pino?

In the meantime, Giorgio had sat back down on his bed.

Do I run quickly toward the exit? I'm not exactly a bolt of lightning, but I should be able to make it.

In the end, one step at a time, sweating bullets, I go over.

"Sit down here," he says indicating a spot next to him on the bed.

I obey.

The way I sit down makes him smile.

"I'm Giorgio." He's missing a canine, the upper left one. He rests his hand on my knee. Sheer terror washes over me.

With a certain clumsiness he bends over to the side, removes a wallet from the back pocket of his jeans and stares into its depths.

"I have a joint in here somewhere. We can smoke it together."

I nod happily, suddenly lightened.

"Sure, whenever you want."

Out comes the crumb of hashish. He places it under my nose. I pretend to smell great aroma, but there was none.

"Did you see what I did to myself?"

"No," I answer.

He turns to me. My smile fades, becomes a wound on my face, everything inside me turns off, and whatever remains alive wants to unsee this.

From afar I hadn't noticed, not even for the whole time I was sitting next to him.

Giorgio shows me his right arm, the one on the far side.

The most ancient line is on the wrist, barely visible, remote

as childhood. Then, one after another, more lines, gradually more distinct. At the height of the elbow they start to become actual scars. On to the upper arm and the powerful biceps until the last one on the shoulder, just sutured, a fresh cut, the blood barely dry. Two stitches close the latest act of self-hate.

I look at the road of gashes without being able to turn my eyes away. I try to count them by tens. There must be at least two hundred, the space in between not more than a few millimeters. The order is approximate; some are half slanted.

"See that?" he asks.

What can I say to him?

I know what I can do for myself: bow my head in front of the ravage. The reason doesn't matter, whether it's right or wrong, but this record-breaking despair merited a tribute of honor.

"Look here, let me show you."

He goes back to fishing around in his worn wallet. He extracts a black-and-white photograph. He positions it in front of my eyes. A fortyish woman, her nice face faded by time.

"This is my mother," he says with the pride of a boy, respectful. Then something inside starts hurting him.

"One morning she says, 'Giorgio, Mamma's going to the market.' I was with Grandpa; I wasn't even ten yet. An hour passes, two hours pass, and Mamma doesn't return. That evening we get a call from the hospital in Genzano."

Giorgio begins sniffling. His hand, still resting on my thigh, begins to twitch.

"Grandpa and I go to the hospital. They take him aside, and he starts screaming like a banshee. They take him away. I stay there with a nurse who asks me what my name is, what my favorite soccer team is, but I want to go with Grandpa, so I run off to follow him. From afar I can hear him still screaming. I get closer. He is looking inside a room, then enters."

Giorgio seems incapable of managing the memory. To him, what he is telling me is not an event that belongs to his past, but it's happening here and now inside of him.

"So I want to enter too, but the nurse blocks me. Then another nurse arrives. I can hear my Grandpa; he can't stop sobbing. I'm almost ten, not a baby, you know. I start yelling to let me in, because I want to see her. But I didn't get to see her anymore."

Inside Giorgio's eyes is the mother they denied him. I can see it through his tears.

"You just don't die like that, without telling anyone, without even saying good-bye to me," he weeps.

He covers his face with his big hand, exhausted.

Now I understand what the cuts along his arm and up his shoulder are. Not the attempts of an aspiring suicide victim like I thought, but a mangling tally. Every time Giorgio experiences the vision of his dead mother, he gashes a line on his skin—as a boy, an adolescent, and a man—like cowboys carve lines on their rifles.

He was not allowed to see his mother, it was denied him, and it turned into a malediction so powerful it locked him in that moment, next to her for eternity, not even ten years old.

I'd like to have a shell, an armor of the best steel, to keep me distant from things. I'd like not to sink into despair over the desperation of others, not to feel as if Giorgio's mother were my mother, as if the life of strangers were wedded to mine by a blood bond.

That's because feeling pain is hard. I'm twenty, but I have suffered for thousands, yet remained the same as before, a child like Giorgio, facing an anguish that you neither fathom nor tame. But children are not made for suffering. They are born from joy, made to live sweetly and cherish all the love that will come their way.

Someone opens the door.

It's Gianluca. He looks in our direction and his face quickly falls.

"Buongiorno," he wishes, but the greeting is only for me, underlined by a rapid batting of eyelashes, not deigning Giorgio even a glance. Maybe they know each other, maybe they were together on some misadventure, the kind reserved only for crazies. Giorgio seems to not notice Gianluca's slight. Gianluca reaches his bed, sits down and continues looking our way, stung like a peeved signora.

Pino walks in without bothering to acknowledge us and starts clearing the cups and what little else was left from breakfast. He stops by my bed.

"You met the harpy last night, eh?"

"Who?" I ask.

"The harpy Rossana. Didn't you see her? She's half witch, always comes by night."

"Seems fine to me," I reply.

"Her? She'd be better off working in a concentration camp. She's a dictator, always been mean."

"She was nice to me. Even gave me a pill, Phenergan. I wouldn't have been able to sleep without it."

"She gave it to you to get you out of her hair, not because she's nice. Having a sleepless lunatic wandering around the ward is a ball-breaker."

Pino is a spontaneous guy, often even friendly, but he does not excel in grace or sensitivity. He is tone-deaf to the lack of regard he has shown me, calling me a lunatic—although I know it's not so far off the mark. Unperturbed, he continues.

"Only good thing about the harpy is that she convinced hospital management to give her the night shift five nights per week, which is totally illegal, but in the end it's good for everybody, especially for me and Dry-Balls."

"Who's that?" I ask.

"Lorenzo, the afternoon nurse. I call him Dry-Balls because

I find him a bit of a wuss. Basically, we have fixed shifts. I do mornings, so I can do odd jobs if I want. Dry-Balls does afternoons, and then he goes out with a girl who I think slaps him around. The harpy works nights, so she can take care of her husband during the day."

"Why, what's wrong with her husband?"

"Had a stroke. Left him like a vegetable, practically. The harpy's with him in the daytime, and their daughter's there during the night. She's even uglier than her mother. Imagine the cheer. Gotta go, still have to finish the breakfast rounds."

Pino and his paunch leave. He makes no effort to seem less indifferent than he is. If there were a championship for unconcern, Pino could have represented Italy.

Good for him. That's how you're supposed to live, with an invisible bullet-proof vest around your heart. Unfortunately, it's a talent that money cannot buy; it's a gift of nature.

"Can we common mortals get the name of the new guest, please?" With Luciferian eyes, Gianluca shoots his request at Giorgio.

"I see that this room is for bros and step-bros getting all friendly while the others are out at the doctor's. Go ahead, keep talking and playing together," he continues, looking in my direction.

"What, you're mad at me now?" I ask him.

Unable to ignore the weak spot he harbors for me, he attempts to drive the point home, but softer now.

"Certainly. I come in and see you two on the bed together. You've never come over to mine, plus he hasn't introduced himself yet." Again he glowers at Giorgio.

"I've lost my soul, Mary! Help me, my little Madonna!"

The yelling makes me jump up from the bed. Next to me, without having made a sound, stands Madonnina. He has woken up.

"I've lost my soul, Mary! Help me, my little Madonna!"

Except for his mechanical supplication, nothing about him communicates a thing, nothing gives a clue.

I look at Mario, then Gianluca, the only two besides me who are equipped with a partially functioning head.

"What do you do in these cases? Call Pino?" I ask.

Gianluca sighs noisily. We've interrupted his outburst.

"Of course. Can't you see he peed his pants?"

I hadn't noticed the stain on his pajama bottoms.

"I've lost my soul, Mary! Help me, my little Madonna!"

I get up and sit him down on a chair, taking him by the wrists. They feel like the wrists of a child. He lets himself be guided without any reaction.

Pino enters.

"Madonnina peed himself," announces Gianluca, reporting the news with the leftover irritation from before. His target is still Giorgio, but the new arrival does not even bother to look at him.

"Basta, I'm putting you in diapers."

Pino's determination as he pulls up Madonnina by the wrist is exaggerated and rude. Usually silent, Mario intervenes: "Careful, you're hurting him."

Even Gianluca has stopped staring at Giorgio because of Pino's hot-headedness. We all look in Pino's direction, at least those of us who are not catatonic.

"I'm not fucking hurting him," exclaims Pino.

"We'll do it if you want, but don't treat him like that," says Mario, his voice louder now. His posture has made the teacher in him visible, and the assertive authority that came with it. In the improvised human recital, Pino is the bratty schoolboy realizing he has overdone it. He drops Madonnina's wrist and takes him more gently by the arm.

"Didn't hurt him one bit," he murmurs. "You people think it's easy. I've been cleaning up piss and shit for twenty-five years. Nobody should be mistreated, as a rule. But what are we supposed to do with someone like Madonnina? He should be in a care home. Instead he's in and out of hospitals, from one to the next. C'mon Madonni'." They exit the room and enter the medical dispensary across the way.

"He does have a point," I say to Mario and look over at Gianluca, too.

Mario remarks, "There's not much rhyme or reason in places like these, but the first thing you need is respect for others. We do a fine job of hurting ourselves without anybody else's help."

No one feels the need to respond. There is total silence, as if Mario's words had made all of us mutely contemplate our respective disorders.

Pino and Madonnina reappear.

"I put his pajamas in bleach, he only has one pair. For now he'll have to stay like this."

Instead of underpants Madonnina has a thick diaper. His naked, slightly bowed legs look like thin branches shriveled in the heat we've been having. Defenselessly, locked up inside himself like always, he lets himself be led back to his bed by Pino.

"Thank you Pino," smiles Mario in an attempt to defuse the friction. The nurse nods and says, "Now let me finish the breakfast rounds. With this, that, and the other, it's almost lunch-time."

At Lake Albano, we boys have a special place for daredevils, for the brave-hearted. It's called the Pope's cabin, a structure made of reinforced concrete, which some say hosted the Holy Father during the 1960 Summer Olympics in Rome. From the cabin, he would have had a prime view of the watersports competitions taking place right there under his summer residence, Castel Gandolfo. In real life, it was some kind of pump house, but maybe something else entirely.

Now it's an abandoned building, perched on a ledge above the lake's crystalline waters.

In our group, barely three or four have the guts to jump. What you do is take a run-up and dive off the edge of the cabin's roof, sailing into the air for at least eight meters. The real risk is entering the water, not just hitting the surface from such a height, but because there's a row of pointy rocks patiently awaiting dudes with poor aim. The water is only safe in a precise zone, maximum a few meters wide. If you mess up, either to the left or to the right, you end up on the rocks, meaning the emergency room, the very same one that gifted me with the involuntary commitment.

The Pope's cabin came to mind looking at the surface of the yellowish liquid in my plate. Beef broth, Pino calls it.

The spoon wants to muster the courage to dive in, but remains suspended, hesitant.

Finally, it makes the swoop.

I can't go on living on cookies alone.

The taste is less terrible than expected.

In these first twenty years as a trainee, I have understood almost nothing about life, but one of the many things assaulting my mind is starting to become clear. Waiting for any type of event becomes for me the worst kind of nightmare. I'd like to be one of those young people who always imagine the best for themselves, triumph after triumph. With me it's the opposite. It's the reason I have never dived off the Pope's cabin and never will. In my eyes, the life ahead is always the worst, so I see myself jumping with surgical precision onto the rocks right beneath the water. I see the rush to the emergency room, the rest of my days a paraplegic in a wheelchair, spoon-fed by my increasingly elderly mother.

Optimism is my secret weapon.

Still, the broth isn't bad. Not like what we have at home, of course, but edible.

The room is a symphony of slurping frenzy. Gianluca is the most delicate. He holds his spoon with his pinky up. Giorgio is the most resolute. His every suck-and-gulp resounds through the whole hospital.

After the last clanging in the plates subsides, my ears fill with entirely different music, a melodic, heavenly Siren song, the enchantment of the postprandial nap. It beckons me, and I would like to give in. My brother and especially my sister both take one. As soon as she lies on a horizontal surface, she literally faints, like one of those dolls with weighted eyelids—whenever you lie it down, it's eyes close. As for me, with my petite stature, small bones and fine hair, I take after my mother, and she doesn't sleep. If she does, it's a light, insipid rest. My father, on the other hand, and his two other children have big bones, a tall frame and wiry hair. He nods off like a hero would after accomplishing an exceedingly arduous feat, even at the table after a meal.

The image of my father poisons my desire for a snooze. I see him again, sprawled on the floor unconscious, his enormous hand squeezed between my eternally childish hands.

My father is a healthy cell in this world, someone who will go down in history, the history of humble people, honest people, untiring workers, family men of the caliber that few are lucky enough to have as a papa and the ones who do, like yours truly, ruin it all.

To hell with taking a nap.

It can't be much after 1:00 P.M.

The ward is too small to take a walk worthy of the name. I could sit in front of the television, but I have no desire whatsoever to do that. This is the hour of news bulletins, something best avoided. I find myself immobile in the middle of the corridor, eager to do something, anything.

In front of me is the double door that leads to the bad patients' department. That definition worries me and at the same time it makes me smile for its coarseness. Good guys and bad guys. It works in primary school, maybe until middle school. I've seen very few truly bad people. I know thieves, drug dealers, junkies, everything the street has to offer, but it's rare that you find a person who enjoys the suffering of others. Usually, the bad we do is out of a wish to serve our interests better and more thoroughly. It's not on purpose, not as a final goal. Let's say the damage procured to the people living around us is a side effect, one that is often taken into account beforehand.

As I lose myself in thought, I arrive at the double door with the obscured glass panes that divides our zone from the malevolent zone.

One could never be sure, but perhaps my mental state is in this condition due to all the curiosity I should have kept to myself. The first instance I remember was when I was around six. A man was lying on the Via Tiburtina, poorly covered by a sheet. I wasn't as shocked by the body as I was by the loafers he was wearing—a pair identical to my father's. I was so upset. Even my father's loafers could die.

We are made of indelible pictures, the background of which becomes blurry over the years. I think of little Giorgio outside of the room that hid his mother's body. Such images can make us leap back in time, and drop us off right there, where the wound was inflicted.

The door is ajar. I push it open a bit, just enough to allow my eyes to do their job. The hand that seizes me by the neck surely belongs to a man.

"You people are really pissing me off today. You know you're not allowed to go beyond this door."

Pino was the ventriloquist, and I was the puppet. He moves me by the neck. His hand turns by 180 degrees, and so do I.

"Now you behave. Are you able to do as I say?"

"Yes," I answer.

Pino loosens his grip. He's wearing his own clothes, ready to leave.

"Sorry, I was bored."

Pino is as quick to cool off as he is to overheat. He scratches his sweaty forehead, puckered by acne scars.

"You could have told me. I would've given you a tour of the hospital, introduced you to the young nurses. Now you go to your room before I kick your ass all the way there."

I see him lunge toward the ward's door, open it with a key, go out, and close it again with me inside, locked up.

In the room, the afternoon nap has won out over everyone except Alessandro and his invincible catatonia. Like with the soup slurping, Giorgio is the most thunderous, snoring like I had never heard it done before. And I've known my share of snorers. Nothing about him is minute or average.

I take from my locker the notebook and pen that my mother had added to the bag my brother brought. I hadn't asked for it; she thought of it, granting my wish before I had expressed it. A mixture of foresight and telepathy.

She was my first reader. For a short while, a girlfriend was my second reader, but now my readership is back to being a single person. She likes my poems, often saying they are sad, but she never stops encouraging me. Really though, how much could a mother's literary judgement be worth?

The pen runs to her. I see her at school, waiting for her son to get out. We were still living in Rome; I was in primary school. My first words written in ink were coming into the world.

"You're always the one to pick me up."

Lorenzo pokes his head into the room, the nurse so affectionately called Dry-Balls by his colleague Pino in an expression of rare courtesy and human delicacy.

"Cimaroli's expecting you."

Writing is strange. To begin, you need a run-up. You need to take a flying swan dive into the white of the page, like my friends at the Pope's cabin. But once you start, you don't want to stop, at least not until that particular electricity generated by everything asking you to be crystalized into words, has run out. When I get interrupted, my thoughts go awry. I imagine the poem I was writing is a lover, abandoned at the height of the moment, offended so much that she leaves forever. As I head out to Cimaroli, I apologize. I don't really know to whom or to what, but I beg their pardon anyway.

"Did you bring me a poem?"

Today Cimaroli is wearing a light blue polo shirt. The very pale skin of his face is lightly tanned.

"No, but I'm trying to write a new one, if I'm able."

"When did you start writing?"

"In the last year of middle school, thanks to my Italian teacher, Ms. Oppes, maybe you know her."

Cimaroli rummages around in his memory, but nothing comes to mind.

"Why thanks to her?"

"In class, she conveyed how important writing can be."

"Tell me about this."

"One morning as she was teaching, she discovers that one of my classmates, Moira Francavilla—I still remember her name—is secretly reading a book on her lap instead of listening to the lesson. Oppes asks her what she's doing. When she sees she is reading a book, she asks for the title. My classmate goes red as a beet. It was the biography of Jon Bon Jovi."

Cimaroli smiles at the name.

"The rock star with the fancy hair."

I nod.

"And so?"

"Instead of getting angry or giving her a note, Oppes asks her to read out loud. Moira doesn't want to, but she has to. It went more or less like this, 'As soon as he arrived in Los Angeles, Jon sweated blood and tears as a barman before getting his first audition.' The teacher lets that sink in, then rushes out of the classroom. We all thought she had gone to the principle's office. Instead, she comes back with a book in her hand, riffles through it until she finds what she's looking for, and gives it to Moira. 'Here,' she says. It was *If This is a Man* by Primo Levi. She makes her read the part where the prisoners are called to the gas showers. They leave the spoon they have been using to the newcomers. The prisoners know they will die, so the spoon is the only thing that will remain of them in the world."

I pause. Maybe because of the nervousness caused by the whole situation I'm in, the memory of that school moment makes it hard for me to not become emotional.

"I might be explaining it badly, but that's when I understood that writing is not child's play, nor is it boring like the way they had taught me. I understood how useful it was, and that it was the only way to recount what I see, what I feel exploding inside me."

Cimaroli has listened attentively. He hasn't once shifted his eyes from my face.

"Why don't you tell me about these explosions inside you, as you call them. I'd like to hear about them," he requests.

I inhale slowly. The doctors' office is definitely hotter than our room. I swipe my forehead; it's wet with sweat.

"It's not so easy. In a nutshell, it would seem as if life were harder for me to face than it is for other people. Not just for the negative stuff, but also for the nice things. Everything seems gigantic to me, but not to the others. I think I might be a bit mentally disabled."

My diagnosis makes him chuckle.

"Disabled, eh? Really?"

"Yes, because the others grow up, become acquainted with death, love, and how life is in general. They accept it, and cohabit peacefully with everything. Not me. I cannot get used to it. Every day I am born all over again, and start learning from scratch. Every night it's as if I were dying, to be reborn in the morning. I suffer from insomnia, maybe that's why. Your colleague yesterday spoke of the alphabet and the ways they teach us at a young age to interpret things. How do we consider someone unable to learn the alphabet? They're disabled, I say."

"You suffer from insomnia?"

"Yes, always have. My mother jokes that it's because I didn't drink milk as a child, but always tea. As if she ever slept."

"Does your mother suffer from insomnia too?"

I nod. "And from anxiety, too. But children are supposed to outdo their parents, right? So I added something of my own."

We remain silent. Cimaroli orders his thoughts, he's reflecting on something.

"Yesterday you spoke of the medicines, the other doctors who took care of you in the past years. What pathologies did they mention?"

"I'm unable to associate doctors with pathologies, but a few spoke of bipolar disorder; one said bipolar something, mixed bipolar disorder, I think; another, Sanfilippo, said I was a borderline case and gave me a medical certificate to bring to the military district. A few months later, I received a letter that was a discharge for illness."

Cimaroli doesn't hide his skepticism.

"Do you remember why my colleagues talked about bipolar depression?"

"Really, the second doctor did nothing but validate the diagnosis of the first, but he tried changing the medicine from Lithium carbonate to Depakene, I think it was called. Whatever. He asked me about my mood in general, and I told him I felt a bit like a plant. In the spring it's as if I were reborn with all the colors, the lengthening days. I experience great joy that lasts all summer, but when autumn comes in September, it's like I'm drying up inside and dying. The melancholy kills me."

"I understand," Cimaroli says, opening a folder. I see my first and last names at the top. Underneath, in big letters, is stamped "Involuntary Psychiatric Treatment."

"It's difficult to make an in-depth diagnosis in one week. Even if I see you every day, which is more or less what we'll do, in order to label it bipolar disorder we'd need a number of instruments that we don't have here. We'd need actual psychodiagnostics."

I'm the one to smile this time.

"Psychodiagnostics? Sounds like something you'd do to a car engine."

"You're right. It's a strange word for a very simple thing, a battery of tests. Neither Mancino nor I have specific competencies in psychodiagnostics. Besides the head physician, who is almost always in the outpatient department on the first floor, we're the only doctors here. Unfortunately, we've been understaffed for over a year now."

"We could go ask the mechanic down at the traffic light," I propose.

The joke hits bulls-eye. When he laughs, Cimaroli's face is truly simpatico.

"Now there's an idea," he admits.

"I'll hook my brain up to the wire so they can read the results on the monitor. Then we'll understand once and for all."

He quickly regains his composure.

"For the moment I'd set aside bipolar depression. I'm more interested in getting you to feel better as soon as possible. Once you've been stabilized, you'll be able to go deeper. You mentioned Anafranil yesterday. That's an anti-depressant as you know, but it's an older, tricyclic type full of collateral effects that you know all about, better than I do. My colleague Mancino referred to serotonin, and I think that should be our departure point. There's a new category of effective psychopharmaceuticals with few side effects. They're called selective serotonin reuptake inhibitors. I think this type of drug might be just the ticket. It doesn't work only for depression, but for all pathologies linked to anxiety, like phobias. It works for obsessive-compulsive disorder too. Do you have compulsions? Do you feel better when you repeat certain actions?"

"Not at the moment. Years ago I had a whole ritual before I ate, having to do with how I washed my hands and such. Nothing special. But as for obsessions, it's different—they practically eat me alive."

"Could you give me some examples?"

The doctors I've met, all of them including Cimaroli, sometimes seem not to acknowledge the enormous quantity of feelings that certain questions unleash in the person who is supposed to answer them. The feelings include a bit of everything, from embarrassment to the difficulty of revealing oneself, and the fear of being taken for more mentally ill than one actually is. But they do not seem to register this.

"They're mostly images, visions. I see my family members dead, almost always in accidents. Or myself losing control. These are the frequent ones, then there are others according to the situation. There's no stopping them. To the contrary, the harder I try to not think of them, the more numerous they become."

"This is another reason to look into SSRIs—that's the abbreviation of the drugs I just mentioned. What do you think?"

"You're the doctor. All I can do is trust you and try to get better. Suffering is terrible, and I'm done with suffering."

"Good. The wish to get better is key."

"I just want to learn to accept life, make it all be normal, like it is for the others."

A girl's screams enter the office without knocking.

It can only be Gianluca.

Cimaroli jumps up to go see, and I'm right behind him.

This is the scene.

Nurse Lorenzo stands between Gianluca and Giorgio.

"I'll cut your throat! Understand? I'll cut your throat!" Gianluca is yelling. Giorgio answers with looks, mostly scornful and provocative.

"If Giorgio raises a hand, he'll smash you like a fly," big boy says, speaking in the third person. He erupts in a giant belly laugh.

"May I know what's going on here?"

Cimaroli addresses Gianluca, the most frenzied of the two.

"Doctor, he says he didn't, but he was looking at me ever since he got here. He's fucking with me. I know right away when someone wants to fuck with me. He called me a hag. Hag, I heard it. Damn him."

Giorgio pretends to be clueless. The pout he puts on is surreal, the expression of a child on the body of a giant.

"Me? Called you hag? Liar. I wasn't even looking at you. You're blaming me because I'm new here. Only person I talked to was him," and he turns toward me. "Right?"

Called into the fray, I nod promptly. "I never even looked at you, I don't know who you are," Giorgio says to Gianluca.

"Go back to your beds and calm down. No more nonsense. I'm not going to repeat this: both of you are here for mandatory care. Remember, the court will be informed of any misdemeanors, so no arguments, no fights."

Hearing the magic word, mandatory, both try to calm down.

"Shake hands and go to your bed, or go watch TV if you want. I don't want to hear any more commotion."

Giorgio sticks out his hand instantly, looking incapable of holding a grudge against anyone. For further confirmation, he adds a smile devoid of the canine on the upper left.

It takes Gianluca a while to reciprocate. When he finally does, he's like a princess awaiting a kiss on the hand. In his eyes, the irritation has not lessened one bit.

"I'll shake your hand, but only because I'm forced to," Gianluca says.

"Good, now behave," Cimaroli ends the discussion and starts heading for the door. He stops, turns toward me.

"I'm sorry Mencarelli, today we were interrupted, but we did get some important things said, didn't we?"

I nod.

"Very good," approves Cimaroli as he swiftly leaves the scene of the battle that ended in a handshake.

During the Giorgio–Gianluca altercation, I kept looking toward Mario to see his reaction. He seems to be the only adult in the room. His back was turned, but every so often he made an attempt to face us, only to go back to his position at the window as if he were afraid, as if the violence being celebrated in the room could somehow reach over and touch him.

Alessandro's father walks in the door. He looks at us without knowing that a second ago a fist-fight was about to break out. His attention is caught by the presence of the new guy, Giorgio.

"Are you new?"

Giorgio nods readily.

"Yes, but they know me well here. I come often."

Alessandro's father sits down next to his son.

And the scene from yesterday repeats itself. The yoghurt comes out of the bag, the little steel spoon wrapped in a paper napkin.

"What's the matter with you?" he asks as he ties a dish-towel around his son's neck, making a bib.

"With me? Nothing. Mamma died, and I did this to myself." He stretches out his arm to show the endless series of cuts, but Alessandro's father doesn't notice, he's absorbed in feeding his son.

"My son was always normal. We worked together. I've been a mason for forty years. He was my assistant. Until one day . . ."

A sudden flash of lucidity.

The mandatory treatment is not the punishment here. If only. The real penalty dealt out by destiny is the reiteration of past experiences, like the re-runs of a show, an eternal theater première. Now we have Alessandro's father reciting his role. This time, Giorgio is the guest of honor.

I cannot stomach another replication of the torment being performed right at the foot of my bed. I rush out of the room faster than if tear-gas had been fired inside.

I find myself roaming the corridor, then start pacing back and forth. I walk in identical, nauseating circles. When I stop, the telephone is beside me.

"Hello."

I wasn't expecting my sister's voice. Usually she's at work at this hour, and if she's not at work she's in her new house as a freshly married bride.

"It's me," I say.

"Mamma is out doing the groceries. How's it going?"

Her voice is strained, distant.

"I'm sorry about what happened, as usual."

Under my sister's silence I hear the sound of the TV, of normal life at home.

"How come you're at Mamma's house?"

I blurt out the question just to break the silence, but it's so naive it's almost a provocation.

"You can't imagine why? But you always had such a lot of imagination."

The implied subject is understood to be my mother.

"How is she?" I ask.

"She's like someone whose son is locked up in a psychiatric hospital."

I wish the guilt burning inside were new, a feeling I'd never experienced before, but it's not. I've been creating problems since primary school. I'm the son who came out of the factory with a defect. I wish with all my heart that this mandatory treatment will be the grand finale of the firework display that was the first 20 years of my life. But something, simply knowing my nature, albeit superficially, tells me it won't be so.

"Sorry, but I have to rush back to work. I just dropped by to say hi to Mamma. If I can, I'll come to see you tomorrow evening," says my sister.

"No. A week will be over quickly. I don't want you or Mamma coming here. Not for any reason."

"Whatever you say."

The phone call home, my sister's voice, it all hits me like a mirage of daily life, light years away from the place where I am.

Cimaroli suggested I take this new class of anti-depressants, but he didn't mention an exact name. If I had the name, I'd pray to it. Instead, on the short hallway of the ward, I invoke medicine generically.

"Holy Medicine, please watch over me and guide me, make me become normal, make me be worthy of my home. Amen."

Madonnina slips by me half naked with his diaper on prominent display, going nowhere, as usual.

Peace reigns in the room now.

Giorgio's probably in the television room, or maybe with the doctors.

Gianluca, for his part, is on his bed trying to apply nail polish to his toe-nails, but something does not convince him. Perhaps it's the color he selected, perhaps his skill in painting it on, or perhaps his masculine feet.

Mario is looking at his tree, still close to his bed. He looks like a prisoner in an invisible magic circle. A spell infuses the few square meters with a different light, infuses him with a different well-being.

"You alright?" I ask. Before I enter his space I want to know if I'm welcome. Mario turns to me and nods yes with an expression of absolute benevolence.

"You?"

"Good enough. I talked to Cimaroli. He advised me to take a drug from a new category of anti-depressants." I look out the window at the big, motionless tree, oppressed by the heat like us.

"Selective serotonin reuptake inhibitors? SSRIs?"

I nod.

"They're pretty clean, not many side effects. Plus they kick in quick. You'll see, you'll feel better for a while."

Mario's words, the last ones, alarm me.

"What do you mean for a while?"

He does not cease looking toward the nest of his bird friend. It's empty. I don't know if it's that or my question, but his natural gentleness wanes rapidly.

"A drug that will cure you does not exist. Neither does one that will be effective on you for life. I already spoke about this with you and I regretted it. You're so young, too young. But what you can find in medicine and from the doctors is at most a small bit of help. The rest is you, the way you see things, the force with which life hits you. Over the years, you'll understand that it's not all bad."

Mario's skepticism sounds pre-packaged, almost ideological. It resembles the talk of certain hippies who live in the woods around the lake. They refuse everything of our times except synthetic drugs.

"Sorry, Mario, if I may ask: why are you here? Here, they prescribe whatever drugs they think best."

He nods. It seems to mean my question is quite pertinent.

"I can't argue with you. I'm here because I need help, like you. Even though I don't believe in it anymore, I have no other choice but to entrust myself to the medical profession. I just want to warn you. I could mind my own business, but you seem to be a nice boy. I'll give you an example. At the school where I taught, from one day to the next, we received calculators instead of the abacuses. Of course I had my pupils use them, but I told them to not stop doing the math in their heads, to not blindly trust those little machines. It's more or less what I'm saying to you: have confidence in the medicine and the doctors, but don't stop working on yourself and doing everything you can to know yourself better. This morning I told you that to me, doctors who study the mind are still like wizards. Then we got interrupted, but I wanted to give you an example. The second—or maybe it was the third—time I was hospitalized, I was sent to a clinic in Palestrina. The mental institutions had been shut down, luckily, not too long before that. The ward was mixed, and in my room there was a woman. She was completely out of her head, and violent. You want to know why? Her son had been diagnosed with autism. Do you know how mainstream science explained that disorder at the time? Do you know what their theory was? It was the child's response to a 'refrigerator mother.' Do you know what that means? According to science, a child became autistic out of lack of maternal warmth. The fault was laid on the mother and her incapacity to love her child properly. Can you believe it? Can you imagine the guilt they felt? What havoc would that wreak on the woman who hears such a thing?"

Mario's account shocks me. Everything seems to be more unhinged than usual, even the floor.

Vainly, he attempts to lighten the mood.

"But those are stories from another era. Science today has improved. I'm old and speak about old folks' stuff. Don't think about it."

His little feathered friend reawakens us. He has materialized in the nest and is looking our way.

We remain motionless, staring at the bird, a small creature animated by life and instinct, nothing else.

When you think about it from another, perhaps more correct angle, diving is always a demonstration of folly. My friends who jump like angels without weight, without death, into the waters of the lake are just plain reckless, devoid of logic. Why jump? Why risk, in the best-case scenario, your life? Too many unknown factors lurk under the water's surface, and very few real advantages, perhaps none. Except for the shouts of glory from us kids. Maybe it's for the adrenaline while it's all being accomplished, suspended in mid-air between life and the rocks.

If logical thinking is what prevails—if knowledge of the dangers becomes the certainty that they will come to pass— you end up not jumping.

I tried this evening. And I failed. Everything suggested danger, the total folly of the dive.

But I was so hungry, and my mother's cookies were finished.

The penne with tomato sauce, presented as so by Lorenzo, were barely worth a glance.

No taste. No consistency.

Eyes closed, they could have been anything.

Mario eats the baked apples we have passed on to him. Giorgio too has adopted the custom. But this evening I'd pay gold to eat mine. An apple is an apple, even if you ruin it.

I finish supper by draining a bottle of apricot juice.

The room's bathroom is quite large. Except for my morning wash, I try to enter it only when strictly necessary. I hate to say it, but everything about it disgusts me, from the odor to the meager personal belongings of the others. When I'm inside, I try to breathe as little as possible. I even have difficulty peeing in there.

To remove the stink from my nostrils, I go breathe in the

corridor. I catch my breath while I cuss this place and myself for ending up here. The second day is not even over yet. An eternity. I'm going crazy in here. Whatever damage I was unable to inflict on myself single-handedly will be accomplished by this mandatory committal.

With my notebook under my arm, I head for the television room. No one is there. I sit down at a table full of old magazines, drawings left by who knows which of the many loonies from the past and present.

On the first page I find the lover I left at the height of everything, and the only verse I wrote.

"You're always the one to pick me up."

I try to go back and synchronize my mind and heart, go back in time to this morning, to the ocean of feelings I had when I used to see my young mother outside primary school waiting for me. I often invented a stomach-ache, a headache, because being far from her was something I could not bear. So many times she came to pick me up before school was out.

Nostalgia is a physical pain. It attacks the middle of the sternum, the lungs.

Well perhaps this thought, written out nicely with the right words, could be an indication, the continuation of my poem. Precisely the word "memory" makes me see how my mind is full of identical scenes: her showing up in the classroom and bringing me home.

At the time, I feigned illness in order to see her. But now, the illness is real, no need to pretend. Only that no one can come get me or take me away.

Gianluca enters the TV room. He's like a radar that registers exactly when the pen is about to hit the paper.

"What're you up to?" he asks.

"Nothing. Wasting time. Drawing."

Immediately I shut the notebook.

"Want to play hangman?" he asks.

Gianluca sits down next to me, his elbow brushes mine.

"You down?" he asks.

I look at him at length. Finally I nod.

"But I go first," he says. He grabs the notebook. I snatch it back. I open it, rip out a page, and give it to him.

He draws the gallows then starts to think.

He picks a rather long word. It starts with a P and ends with an E.

I soon end up being the stick figure hanging from the gallows drawn by Gianluca. All I added to the secret word is an A.

PLEASURE.

Gianluca observes the word for quite some time. Having formed it and seeing it handwritten on the paper has a strange effect on him. He seems to lick his lips. He looks at me and realizes he has gone too far.

"Anyway, your turn now," he says.

I start thinking of a word. Finally, I find one. It's shorter than his.

ESCAPE.

"Lights out, signori."

Rossana peeks into the room rapidly.

I beam a broad smile at her. It's a request, not so veiled, but she pretends not to see me. I rush from my bed.

"Excuse me."

I follow her down the hallway.

"Excuse me."

Finally she stops, but does not turn around. I quickly catch up to her.

"Good evening. I wanted to ask you for last night's sleeping pill, Phenergan. It really helped."

She starts shaking her head no.

"I am sorry. I left a note for the doctors, but Cimaroli wrote to me saying that you're not allowed to have sedatives or sleeping pills. I can't help you."

This time the enterprise seems truly complicated. Pino's words come to mind.

"So we won't tell him. Isn't it better that I sleep? I'm thinking of you. I'll be up wandering around the ward all night, otherwise," I say.

She takes a closer look at me, from my slippers to the ends of my hair. What she sees molds her face into a condescending expression.

"Do whatever you want, but I'm not giving you a pill. Good night."

For Rossana, the discussion is over.

She is not the target of my hatred, but that bastard Cimaroli. Tomorrow I intend to find out why exactly he's not giving me a sleep aid. As I throw myself back on my bed, drained and damp from all the day's sweat, I cannot stop thinking about him. Cimaroli is probably on his terrace waiting for dinner to be served, because out there in the normal world, it's still early. He's sipping half a glass of wine, far removed from his patients and the entire ward. Then I imagine him in his jogging suit, running (or trying to) on the path along Lake Albano.

I don't know if it's thanks to their meds, but everyone is already asleep in the room except Gianluca. I'm sure of Giorgio; he's snoring blithely albeit with less vehemence than this afternoon, perhaps due to his position.

Mario lies turned toward the tree. His lack of movement and regular breathing suggest he's asleep.

Alessandro is still looking at his secret spot above my bed, but he doesn't really count. It's incredible how human beings are able to get used to things, even the most bizarre and unlikely of them. Across from me I have a young man looking at nothing, completely still, all day and all night, like a broken robot. But I almost don't notice it anymore. My initial incredulity and amazement are gone, leaving no trace.

Madonnina's eyes are closed, his skeletal profile pointing up to the ceiling. I'm not sure if it's simply my imagination or the fact that I am a bit closer to him now, but as soon as I glimpse his diaper I smell a bad odor. It would seem that no one has changed it or washed him.

Gianluca, the only one awake, has been putting his locker in order for quite some time. He's folding clothes and neatening his space like a good housewife.

I start my sleep ritual.

I repeat to myself that I will make it. I smile to calm myself. This night is going to be easy. I try to give order to my breathing, then I concentrate on something that is nice and calming at the same time. Mario's birdie comes to mind. I imagine myself in the nest with the bird. We're sleeping peacefully in the fresh breeze that rocks the boughs and cradles us. I wonder if there are insomniacs among the animals. Their sleep is different from ours. It's light. They remain vigilant, but in their own way they sleep. Insomnia is different, it's a pathology, it's an unfulfilled wish to sleep, it's wakefulness that refuses to subside.

It always ends up this way.

The pleasant Arcadian image doesn't last. My mind worms its way in even there, transforming the picture into reflection, interrogation. And I fall for it.

I rise.

Sitting in the only worn and tattered armchair in the television room is Rossana. She sees me come in and does not hide her displeasure.

"May I?" and I sit down next to her. Maybe my presence, the obvious annoyance, will make her change her mind about the Phenergan.

The TV is on the Rai Uno channel.

"What's on?" I enquire.

"*Un disco per l'estate*. But if you're going to stay here, be quiet."

The program kicks off with a bang. The first guests are the band Corona with *The Rhythm of the Night*. I can't stand commercial Eurodance. I like techno; now that's music. The song doesn't seem to do much for Rossana either.

"Pino bad-mouthed me, didn't he?" she asks without unsticking her eyes from the TV set, gazing disgustedly at the Corona performance. My silence makes her turn to me.

"You can tell me, don't worry. I know he does it to everyone."

"Not exactly bad, but he made some remarks."

"He said I'm ugly and old, right?"

I remain mute, acquiescing.

"Let me tell you the truth. We were hired here together twenty-five years ago. Both of us were single. He fell in love right away, flirting constantly. But I liked the guy I ended up marrying. Pino was unable to accept that, and over time he became nasty about it."

"Of course," I comment. I really don't know which of them is telling the truth, and I couldn't care less. I show that I'm on her side because I hope she'll change her mind about the Phenergan.

A scream of desperation freezes us. The scream of a woman.

Out of fright, I grab Rossana's wrist.

We remain motionless, listening.

After a moment of perplexity, she regains her composure.

"Is that coming from the bad people?" I ask.

Rossana nods.

"Aren't you going to check?"

"They have their own night nurse. They are entirely separate from here; even their entrance is on the other side. Better that way, believe me."

The scream, plus the idea of watching songs on television that I detest, makes me get up and head for the only place I'm allowed to go.

I don't even bid Rossana good night.

I'm back in the room.

I don't have a watch, but it can't be after ten.

I try closing my eyes. But I can't close my nose.

As the hours pass, the air in the room becomes a lethal mix. It's unbreathable.

From Madonnina's diaper to Giorgio's gigantic feet; from Gianluca's bleached hair to Mario's winter robe; it even includes the nothingness forcibly shoved inside Alessandro.

The air is heavy with their cursed insanity. It's incurable, neglected and abandoned.

Rage knows how to seduce. It's calling me. I feel it expanding through my veins. It's heating my forehead. I'm invaded by it.

There is nothing in here that I do not hate profoundly.

I hate all of you. For what you are.

But even more for what you represent.

The vision of what could be.

The incarnation of my future.

This is what's waiting for me.

I hate you all.

I hate myself.

DAY 3
THURSDAY

It's just after dawn when the breakfast is served.

I'm the first to wake, after having been the last to fall asleep.

Then it's Mario's turn. Straight away, his gaze runs to his tree.

"Today, every one of you has to hit the showers. Can't breathe in here."

Pino's morning salute is loud and clear.

One gulp of tea and I'm off.

I enter the bathroom with my towel under my arm, determined to get this over with as quickly as possible.

I instantly enter the stream of water. It's freezing. Suddenly it's boiling. I spend useless minutes trying to regulate the temperature. In the end I opt for freezing. At least I know what to expect.

In front of the mirror, I notice my beard has grown. But the side of my head lapped by Madonnina's fire is still shiny. The hair has not started sprouting, at least from what I can tell from the dim, badly lit mirror.

Thanks to the water, the bandage on my left hand has softened. I slowly peel it off. A series of small cuts, scratches and bruises is covered by tincture of iodine.

In all, it took me ten minutes at most. When I get back in the room, the other patients are all busy with breakfast.

"Mamma mia, you smell so good!" Gianluca says, coming close. He slides the bottle of shower soap out of my hand.

"Can I borrow this? So we have the same scent."

"As long as you don't finish it," I say.

He's so happy he hugs me.

Then he pauses. Seeing Giorgio's mouth full of rusk, his face falls immediately.

"Well, I guess I'll go take a shower."

Gianluca disappears into the bathroom.

With a flick of my head I greet Mario, who reciprocates at once. I do the same with Giorgio, who smiles, offering me a good look at that rusk he's eating.

"We go smoke that little joint later, okay?" he asks.

I scowl at him.

"Why don't you put up a sign? So if people didn't hear you, they can read it there." But he is unable to appreciate my sarcasm. So I lean closer to his bed.

"Lower your voice. If they find you with a joint, you'll get into trouble."

"Ah," he says.

My bed is completely wet. I see Pino out in the hall and run after him.

"Pino, excuse me." He seems to not hear me.

"Hey! Pi'!" I shout. That forces him to stop.

"Could you change the sheets today? Mine are soaked."

He takes note of the request.

"After lunch, when Lorenzo's here. I'm not about to change all the beds alone."

"All right, we seem to have no engagements after lunch."

He sniggers, "What, you trying to be funny?"

"I try," I answer.

He pretends to smack me across the face, then slips into the medical dispensary, leaving me alone in the corridor.

From the blaring television comes the weather report. There's an overview of Italian cities, where people are shown wiping perspiration from their brow, and others are swimming in the sea or a pool. The commentator is almost relishing the announcement of record high temperatures. Today and tomorrow will be the peak of this heatwave. I change channels, roaming around with the remote, but there's not one program that interests me. I have two places where I can be: this room and my room. I dry my sweat. Last night's rage is still with me, ready to reconquer me. I remain where I am with the TV off. I could do some writing, take up my poem, but I don't feel like it now. I just want to get out of here, go to the lake with my friends, and kick-start some magnificent, furious goofing around. But I am not like them. I've always known. For now I am able to hide life's wounds, but I won't succeed in doing it forever.

In the room, the scent of my bath foam covers every other smell. It stinks. Gianluca hands me the bottle without having the courage to look at me. It's practically empty.

"It fell. I'm sorry."

I see on his face the girl he carries inside. She is embarrassed, mortified.

"It's okay. At least now it smells nice in here."

Gianluca agrees, and returns to his boundless cheer.

"Yes, can you smell how sweet? It's like we're in the mountains!"

He opens his arms wide, as if standing in a rolling Alpine meadow where the breeze ruffles the wild flowers.

Mario has been watching, and he too smiles at the unrestrained expression of joy. Shyly, with his head down, Giorgio comes over and asks me, "You wouldn't lend your soap to me, would you? All I have is toothpaste and a toothbrush."

I hand him the bottle.

"Here, hope it's enough."

Giorgio is in seventh heaven.

"Thanks, bro."

The pat on the shoulder he gives bends me over sideways. He is unaware of his own strength.

"Let's go Mencare'. Mancino's expecting you."

I turn toward Pino's voice.

"What Mancino? You mean Cimaroli."

"Think you know better than me? If I say Mancino, it's Mancino. Let's go."

Mario waves to me as I exit the room.

In the corridor with Pino next to me, I find myself musing upon Mario's kindness and spontaneous goodness.

"Mario's really a nice guy. Smart, too. You'd never say he deserves to be in here."

Pino stops, lets my words sink in, then has trouble holding in his laughter.

"You, Mencare', certainly have a lot of insight. You can really tell you're twenty years old. Haven't understood shit about life." It's not because of the offense to me, but for the allusion to Mario that I come to a halt in the hall.

"Now tell me why I don't understand shit about life and about Mario."

Pino would like to move on, but notices my total resoluteness. This time, I'm not going to budge if he doesn't talk.

"In your room, there's only one patient who can be dangerous. Guess who?"

I remain speechless.

"No," I say.

Pino nods vehemently.

"None other than him. He's been on trial for attempted murder. Wife and daughter."

"What the fuck are you saying?"

"Then the wife withdrew her complaint and everything came to a stand-still. But he's not allowed to see them, not even from a distance. Do you hear me? Let's go, Mancino's waiting."

I enter the doctor's office full of resentment. Toward Mario, toward this place. Mancino's ceremonial smile is the icing on the cake. There is no longer a shred of rage in my body. Now melancholy is in command. A sense of defeat, unconditional surrender, makes me sit down like an empty sack.

"Isn't Cimaroli here?"

"He's held up in the emergency room for a consultation."

We remain in silence. I have no desire to speak, and he has no desire to show me he wants to listen or even pretend to listen out of duty, like he did last time.

"So? How's the vacation going?" is Mancino's first question after several minutes. I'm not sure it merits a response. If I had to tell the rugby player who mistakenly became a psychiatrist the truth, I'd say more or less the following: "Dear Doctor Shit-head, I am not on vacation but committed to mandatory psychiatric treatment. I spend my vacations wherever I want, taking advantage of the most precious thing we humans have after life: freedom. Something you have taken away from me at the moment, with the approval of the municipality where I reside and the Tribunal of Velletri."

I'd season my words with a head butt right on his mouth.

"Great. It's really hot, perfect for a vacation," I end up saying instead. He does not acknowledge my quip. Whatever I do or say does not interest him. I'm just a speck of dust to him, nothing important.

"Cimaroli's not here, so I'm asking you: why did you take away the Phenergan? I can't sleep in here."

Mancino sighs, flicks through my folder.

"Nothing written here."

"But the nurse, Rossana, told me he wrote it down."

Mancino's reaction is to turn the folder toward me.

"I am unable to find anything, so you check," he says.

I decline his challenge.

"If you have no further requests, I'd like to ask you something," he says. "This was written in your folder by Cimaroli. I'll let you check if you want. Or do you trust me?"

I open my arms, go ahead.

"Cimaroli jotted down a question in pencil here. He wanted to ask you about your relationships. Do you have a girlfriend at the moment?"

Having made his enquiry, he leaned long into the chair's backrest with his arms crossed, waiting for my words.

I see all my girlfriends in front of me, from age fourteen to the last one, who was twenty like me.

"I don't have one now. I've had a few. Most of them ran for the hills when they understood who they were dealing with."

"What do you mean, ran for the hills? Why? What did you do to them? Did you let your hands wander?"

I make a disgusted face. Mancino's words always allude to the worst.

"Never touched a girl in my life. They were the ones who beat me up. Especially one. When we argued, she'd kick me. I mean they made themselves scarce because of my reactions, certain types of over-the-top behavior."

"Give me some examples."

Memory begins its selection process. The first recollection makes me laugh. That thing I did to Alice, that was her name, was really extreme.

"I bought a ring for one of my first girls. One afternoon we start fighting. After a while, I tell her, 'Give me the ring back.' She takes it off and I swallow it, but the ring sticks in my throat and I almost suffocate. The poor thing, she was crying, terrified."

The first memory is followed by the fragment of another, completely different one, one of happiness as pure as a diamond. I experience the moment again and suddenly it makes me cry.

"But they're not necessarily bad things. The good things were huge, too." I stop to fight back the tears. "The one I loved most of all was called Carolina. One evening we were driving on Via Cristoforo Colombo without a destination. We liked to drive around aimlessly, just to hang out together, talk. At a certain point, she smiles. It was so much of everything. So I tell her that when she smiles at me like that, it makes me love not only her, but everything in the world, even the billboards, even the street lamps—the ones on Colombo are really enormous. So to show her what I mean, I stop the car, hop out and throw my arms around a lamp-post. I stand there hugging it for I don't know how long."

My past flashes in front of my eyes like one single, gigantic lost opportunity, sacrificed on the altar of the way I am and the way I see things. I snap out of it. I wearily return to the doctor's office, to my interlocutor. Mancino has listened attentively, with his eyes closed. Then I look again, more carefully.

Mancino doesn't move, doesn't speak. I might be mistaken. I try to know for sure. I clear my throat. I cough.

Now I am sure.

Mancino has fallen asleep.

"Doctor."

Pretty deeply, too. You can tell by his breathing. It's slowing down. He soon starts snoring, even.

I feel sorry for myself. I do not rouse clinical curiosity. As a mental patient I do not even reach mediocrity.

Absurd envy mixes with my ruefulness. It's just as inappropriate as the reason that makes me feel it. It's neither for his status nor for any other motive attributable to his role as a headshrinker. What I'm jealous of is Mancino's natural ability to fall asleep on a chair, an unstable chair. A person capable of sleeping in such conditions is a master of the universe.

Gradually, all this is joined by a feeling of hate, massive spite, hard as granite.

I rise from my chair. The move finally rouses him from his angelic repose. He does not lose his composure, does not feel the need to give me an explanation.

"You were asleep," I say, thinking, hoping, to embarrass him, but that doesn't happen.

"I wasn't asleep. A doctor's detachment from his patient's words is part of the therapeutic approach."

I'd really like to answer him the way he deserves, but I don't have the strength to do anything. I just want to leave.

"Okay, are we done?"

Mancino nods, looks at me closely. He's indecipherable.

"I'm not the sentimental type. I leave that up to Cimaroli. Just remember one thing. It makes no sense to treat the brain differently from the rest of the body. If you have an ulcer, what do you do? You cure the ulcer. If you're mentally ill, you have to cure the mind. The rest is just psychobabble. Cure yourself. You still have time, if you don't want to end up like the rejects you have in your room."

I leave the doctor's office dazed. I don't feel anything. I don't want anything. Mancino has transmitted the feeling he has toward me. Something similar to a zero.

Who forces people like him into the medical profession? Where did his calling go, the calling that made him choose to become a doctor? Can a university degree, economic survival and social status justify such unhappiness?

Because he is the unhappy one. We patients sit with him at most for one hour per session, but he's the one who has to live with himself and his dissatisfaction day after day for his entire life.

Although I'm only twenty, I am not naive. I have known dozens and dozens of shrinks and other doctors. I'm not asking for saints gifted with extraordinary clinical perspicacity, but I don't want men who are disaffected with themselves and the entire human race, either.

The spectacle offered to my eyes when I go back to the room is surprising, to say the least.

Giorgio, washed and smelling like my shower soap, is sitting on Gianluca's bed. The two are chatting like old acquaintances.

"Hey Danie', come see how good Giorgio smells now."

Giorgio reacts by getting up from the bed and coming over to me. He bends down to bring his neck to my nose.

"Smell," he says proudly.

But I am in no mood to have fun, smell perfume, participate in things that involve other people's lives.

Gianluca notes my lack of reaction. He takes a closer look at me.

"Hey, Danie', what'd you do? You seem like Madonnina."

Mario has turned toward me too. He's another one on my list, acting like a great wise man and then he goes and tries to kill his wife and daughter.

But my wish to share my bitterness with someone is too strong. If I keep it inside, it'll explode in a different way. Maybe it'll become rage, and I can't allow that to happen in here.

"Mancino fell asleep while I was talking to him." Everybody is listening to me. I can't be sure Alessandro and Madonnina are, seeing their state.

"I was speaking of something close to my heart, and there he was, sleeping like a baby. They help you fall down more than they lift you up in this place."

They are absorbed by my words. Gianluca gets up, comes to me, and hugs me tightly, too tightly.

"Oh honey, you're going to meet many of them. I had one—you needed a brass band to wake him up."

Giorgio and Mario show comprehension and sympathy.

"Most of them work twelve hours per day, because they have private practices and hospital work. They're only human."

Mario's comment doesn't help me. I look at him resolutely.

"It's not like God Almighty tells them to do it. It's their choice."

His invisible antennae pick up on my resentment. He bows his head without replying.

I head toward him with visible rancor, riled up by Mancino, riled up by everything I've experienced in these days. I point my finger at Mario.

"People in this room think they have all the solutions for the others. They think they have something to teach us. If only they'd mind their own fucking business!"

What I see next is something my eyes had never set sight on in my life.

Like a sponge, Mario absorbed all my bad blood. The words I aimed at him have made him buckle, more than if I had struck him. I regret it, every single bit of it, having crushed him like this. He is defenseless and trembling. He looks like a trapped animal, cornered between his bed and the window.

"I'm sorry," I utter, not knowing what else to say.

He nods mechanically. He turns toward a plastic cup full of water and drinks it slowly. My eyes run to the tree, to his feathered friend's nest. He's there. His black pearls have seen everything.

"The little bird is there," I say.

Mario looks out the window.

We stay that way for a while.

The heat licks our face like flames.

"Pino told me. About your wife and daughter."

I do not want him to think that my words were gratuitous, that I hurt him just for the hell of it. Now at least he knows that it was a reaction, pain transformed into more pain.

"Next month I turn sixty-four. I've lived for many years. I've understood a few things. Other things I have not. For instance I have understood that intelligence is overrated, like stupidity is underrated, that good and evil really exist, and that humans can waste their precious time in thousands of stupid ways. The most stupid way is judging others, because it's too easy, because it's no use to us or the others."

Suddenly I see myself in all my presumption. The finger I pointed at Mario like a gun aimed at an innocent person. Precisely me, I did that. Me, who earned this mandatory commitment for having almost killed my father.

A little at a time, Mario returns to his old self, with his treasure of humanity to share with whoever wants it.

"Look around you. All of us are victims and tormentors of ourselves. What Pino told you is true. It happened many years ago. Back then, the evil was unbearable. I had just been placed in retirement for ill health. I was unable to go forward, and support the family I loved. When men cannot protect, they begin to destroy. Animals do it too. And so I started destroying what I adored. One night I almost ended everything. My wife and my daughter left me. They made the right choice. Now I show them my love by keeping far away from them."

We let more time pass in silence, looking at life moving inside the little bird. He's going about his business, thinking his mysterious thoughts without needing to tell us anything else.

Carrying a basin full of water, Pino enters the room.

"I'm going to get this over with before lunch."

Armed with a sponge, he starts washing Madonnina, one arm at a time, then one leg at a time. When he removes the diaper, I turn away.

Madonnina lets Pino work. I look at his eyes. They are staring at the ceiling. They are immensely similar to the ones of Mario's bird. Illegible, lively with obscure life, inaccessible to the human race.

"Little thing, come, give me a hand," says Pino.

The "little thing" is me. He has me lift Madonnina by the shoulders so he can wash his back.

I can't be sure, it might have been the position, because my face is a hand's breadth from his pointy nose, but for a moment I had the impression that he was looking at me intently. It was like a flash of lucidity in his eyes, immediately swallowed by the black fog that envelops them from inside.

I did not have lunch.

Despite the fact that the rice with tomato sauce looked decent.

Today is the third day of involuntary treatment, the worst until now.

Heightening my discomfort is the overwhelming heat. It's probably after two o'clock. If I were at my house, I would have taken my second shower of the day now. I left the room with the others trying to rest, but the heat made it a difficult enterprise even for them.

The short hallway was a rectangle of five meters wide and ten meters long. On the walls hung color photographs of towns in the environs, two pictures for each of the long walls. Albano Laziale. Genzano di Roma. Ariccia. Castel Gandolfo. I spent my whole life in these towns. The schools. The soccer fields. The friendships. The falling in love. A tiny plot is my universe. I have never loved these places as much as now, at this moment: their indisputable beauty and marvelous conjunction of history and nature. It is no coincidence that they have been vacation and travel destinations for 2,000 years. And now I find myself in this rectangular hallway with four photos on the otherwise all-white walls. Well, "white." There's dirt everywhere. Suddenly my throat tightens claustrophobically. I feel imprisoned inside an enormous coffin with a white interior. A coffin underneath a thousand meters of earth with the oxygen about to finish.

The sound of a bell ringing makes me jump, but nobody seems to notice it. Lorenzo is probably busy with other duties.

Another ring, slightly longer than the first.

I open the door.

One centimeter from my face stands my father.

His astonishment is greater than mine.

The last time I saw him he was sprawled on the floor in the middle of the living room, and my heart was pierced by the terrifying thought that I had killed him.

We stand there looking at each other, each making a special inventory of the other. My father stops at the height of my hair, stretches out his hand toward the bald spot without a word.

"A guy in my room, poor devil. But it's all under control."

It takes me much effort. I have to chase away the shame beyond my conscious mind before I succeed.

"How are you?" I ask.

My father opens his arms as if to say, "Look at me."

"I'm on my feet, see?" he says.

We embrace right at the door to the ward.

"I'm sorry," I tell him. I'd spend my life saying it. Not only for having almost killed him the other night, but for everything I did until then, for what I might still do because of my half-crazed head.

My father takes a step toward me. He wants to come in, but I don't budge.

"No, Papa. Better you don't. It's monstrously hot. I prefer staying out here at the door." I know that the heat is only one of the reasons I don't want him to come in. He acknowledges my wish, and adapts.

"How do you feel?" he asks.

"Except for the hair, everything's fine. There's a good doctor. They did the right thing making me stay here for a week. You'll see, this time they'll finally get to the bottom of what's wrong with me."

"What are you doing there by the door?" shouts a voice, echoing through the corridor. It's Lorenzo. He looks out of the dispensary, alarming both my father and me.

"My father came to see me." He bounds over.

"Never open that door without permission! Understood?"

"But it kept ringing and no one came to open it."

"You let it ring. Patients are not allowed to open the door. Plus, this is not visiting hour!"

My father speaks to me with his eyes. He's telling me to let it go. Mechanically he hands me a bag. Inside are cookies, bottles of water and a magazine.

"I'm leaving now, don't worry," he says, trying to calm him down. Lorenzo's response is a hard look full of superiority and conceit. You wouldn't even look at a dog that way.

My father and I embrace again.

"We'll talk by phone. Tell Mamma I'll call her tomorrow."

Another embrace.

I close the door.

I was still a child the first time I found myself hugging my father with this strange sensation clenched between my jaws. That hug seemed to me to be the last. Like a goodbye. A farewell. After that first time came millions of others. With him. With my mother. With everyone I cherished and wished to protect. Why do I have to live with this curse? Like everybody else in here, I am my own condemnation. Each of us has an obsession to carry out infinitely.

With my eyes fixed on the white of the ceiling, I repeat the word, accessible to only me. I don't even say it to my mother. It is my obsession, my pathological desire.

Salvation.

From death. From pain.

Salvation for all my loved ones.

Salvation for the world.

In the meantime, Lorenzo has walked off.

He's about to enter the dispensary again. I jog over to him.

He finds before him the worst version of me.

The rage climbs over every single cell. It arrives at my

pupils, dilates them. I feel my strength multiplying a hundred-fold in my muscles. My veins are pumping blood.

"You were rude." I can tell him what I had to swallow with Mancino. Lorenzo tries to not be intimidated. He'd like to continue on his way, but I step in front of him.

"You're rude now too. I am talking to you and you don't stop walking."

Outside, in normal-people life, I would have already shoved him against the wall. But with the crumb of lucidity I have left, I force myself not to touch him, on any account. The Tribunal of Velletri is the bogeyman flying around my head.

"You can say things politely, you know. Don't you dare do that again. Hear me?"

I can't tell if it's my shuddering chin, the sweat dripping from my forehead, or my hands fluttering in front of his face, but he, Dry-Balls, nods timidly now.

"Yes. I'm sorry. Sorry."

He hurriedly disappears into the dispensary.

I have to escape.

But I cannot do it physically.

I only have one way to get myself out of here, to change the horizons of my mind. My imagination.

I retreat into the empty page to translate into words the memory of my mother.

With the notebook under my arm, I go to the television room. I sit at the table. I face the wall, turning my back to the real world.

First, I rip out all the pages. I transcribe the only verse I birthed onto a blank page.

"You're always the one to pick me up."

The moment has come to make myself vulnerable to life, without my defenses, arms open wide, as naked as the day I was born.

Here she is. She reappears in my mind with her plaid coat, the black hair of youth, the smile of a mother reunited with her child.

I let myself be transfixed, pierced by the memory like a convict kissing his torturer on the mouth.

My mind enters its abyss. My eyes probe inside my skull.

When I touch the inner apex of things, there is sudden clarity. Words of flesh and blood come out of the ground.

When I re-emerge, the smell of soup, the sun lower, the tiredness of a trip just concluded.

In the notebook are pages and pages of words, written and crossed out, rewritten and crossed out again. Verses loved, hated one second later, and thrown away.

On the last page, in my elementary left-handed handwriting, is the poem to my mother and to my pain—the pain of these days and the pain of always.

I read it one last time, tasting its melody, consistency and internal tension.

I smile.

At the end of the work, I thank her, poetry, for having come to visit me once again.

The dinner they left on my nightstand is cold by now. It makes no difference. I would not have touched the soup they served even if it had been scalding. I do not despair, because my father has replenished my ammunition of chocolate cookies.

I see Alessandro's father in the room. He has finished feeding his son. Now he is combing his hair. I see something that makes me curious. His left arm is under the covers and his hand is squeezing his son. Probably a gesture of affection. Alessandro's father notices me staring. I try to pretend I'm not. I reach for one of the packs of cookies I have placed on my nightstand. He has removed his arm.

"Every now and then I give him a pinch to see if I can wake him up."

Alessandro's father looks in my direction.

"He seems to be sleeping with his eyes open. What if he stays this way? What disorder is this? He's not alive and he's not dead."

Despite the increasingly muggy heat, a shiver travels down my spine.

I imagined Alessandro a prisoner inside himself, sane, conscious, able to hear all his father's desperation, and feel his pinches that try to waken him. He wants to shout, wants to tell the world about his imprisonment, but disability impedes his ability to command what used to be his body, his mouth. I get up from my bed like a robot. The idea of getting stuck inside myself might just be the worst vision I've ever imposed upon myself—going mad inside a body turned prison, a cell made to measure for lunatics, with padded walls. An invisible strait jacket. You witness the torment of people suffering because of your condition without being able to do anything.

I'm back in the television room.

On Italia Uno, there's the program *Karaoke*. There's not a living soul in the room except me. I turn off the TV. I go to the window. There's a very nice view I hadn't noticed. On the horizon in the distance lies the sea. But the haze takes a big part of the panorama's beauty away. Probably because the window faces the sea, every now and then I feel something similar to a thin breeze wafting in.

"Good evening." Rossana takes possession of the worn armchair. One second later, she turns on the TV.

"You told me Cimaroli took me off the Phenergan, but there's no mention of in in my folder. I checked."

"Who told you he wrote it in the folder? He left the note for me on a sheet of paper."

Rossana's answer leaves me without a leg to stand on. There

is no glimmer of hope. A second taxing night looms, the pursuit of sleep amid cries and delirium of all shapes and colors.

Miserably I return to my room. At least now it smells wonderful, especially thanks to my shower soap. The bottle reposes empty and capless in the garbage can to the side of the door.

Mario has washed too. I notice it from his curly hair, less weighted down and greasy than this morning. His pajamas, on the other hand, have remained the same as always.

I place the notebook with my poem in the drawer of my nightstand. Tomorrow I'll read it to Cimaroli. I lie down. The bed is amazingly hot, as if warmed by a hidden fire.

Right above his bed, Gianluca has attached a paper with a smiling sun. The drawing is basic, but if the intention was to cheer up the room, I can say it does its task just fine. In this sweltering heat, however, I would have portrayed the sun with a satanic sneer instead of a smile.

The toilet flushes. Giorgio comes out of the bathroom. He has exchanged his undershirt for a white T-shirt with a stylized parrot at the height of the chest pocket. The shirt's one size too small. The right sleeve is rolled up. I imagine this is to show off the trail of slashes, although he doesn't seem to be the exhibitionistic type. Maybe he rolled it up to allow the most recent gash, the fresh one, to breathe and heal over.

"You like it, Danie'? I gave it to him."

Gianluca looks at what used to be his T-shirt with a blend of pride and satisfaction.

"Yes. It looks good on him."

Drawn into the exchange by my words, Giorgio swells like a peacock.

Each of us takes possession of his own bed.

It's lights out. Gianluca does the honors. He's the closest to the switch.

"Mamma mia, it's so hot. And I'm close to the window,"

says Mario, giving a voice to everyone's discomfort. He's sitting with his back against his pillow.

"My God, really. My hair's wet," Gianluca says, grasping the red lock he uses to cover his bald spot. He lifts it off his scalp like a mohawk. Now he looks like a post-apocalyptic punk.

This night, sleep evades everyone except Madonnina and Alessandro, but they no longer belong to the category of the living whose life is divided into sleeping and waking hours.

"You complain about Mancino, Danie'. In my twenty-five years of mental disorders I've come across some real sons of bitches, especially one. He had a heart of stone. His name was Bonafede, which is supposed to mean 'good faith,' except he had none. I was really young, crying all the time. I asked for help. But he'd get angry because my tears wet his desk. It had belonged to his father and his grandfather."

As he spoke, Gianluca tended to his long comb-over, smoothing it once again perfectly over the bald part of his skull.

Giorgio, Gianluca's T-shirt taut over his chest, speaks looking at the ceiling: "One doctor gave me so many pills I slept for an entire week. To wake me up, my grandfather would prick me with a pin, but I didn't even feel that. When he was still alive, he was the one who talked to the doctors. They didn't bother to talk to me, said I was demented."

I ask Mario, "What about you? What's the worst doctor you've had?" His life seems an unattainable sum of experiences. He starts thinking, going back in time.

"I've known doctors who used to work in insane asylums. They were used to restraint and verbal and physical violence. But there wasn't one in particular. Most of all there were the ones unable to really listen, who think there is nothing to learn from a person they judge to be mentally ill. But it's too long a story."

"We have all night," Gianluca answers, opening his arms to show the size of the hours ahead of us.

Mario gives him an affectionate look.

"I've been frequenting places like this for over 40 years, and I notice how the concept of mental disorder is spreading. A kind of race is on nowadays to put the label of disorder on things that until a short while ago were simply a person's characteristics, sometimes even considered virtues. Science is invading ambits that used to not belong to it. Today, a youth who has questions about life, death and God is answered by means of medicine. There is immediate talk of depression. Until 50 or 100 years ago, that youth would have been sent to a priest, or far from home to cut his teeth."

Still with his back against his pillow and his arms crossed, Mario looks in my direction. I feel that the youth who appeared in his words is me. He's talking to me.

"I'm not saying mental disease does not exist, that's not true. I've known psychos who'd send shivers up your spine, people who took pleasure in other people's pain. But today, mental illness is not the only thing being treated. Today, it's the enormity of life, the miracle of an individual's uniqueness. It unsettles people, so science wants to contain and catalogue. Everything's considered a malady now. Did you ever ask yourselves why that is?"

Mario asks us with his eyes, but no one answers.

"A man interrogating himself about life is not a productive man, that's why. He might start suspecting that the latest fashionable pair of shoes that he wants so badly is not going to take his malaise away. The shoes are not going to temper the dissatisfaction gnawing at him from inside. A man contemplating the limits of his existence is not sick. He's simply alive. If anything, it's craziness to think that a man must never know a crisis."

"Mario, of course what you say is true, but I am bipolar, I really am. The problem is that the frigging doctors are unable to find efficient remedies. Yes, you feel better for a little, but then you have to start all over again," says Gianluca. It's the same objection I have.

Mario has listened attentively.

"True, you're bipolar, I'm psychotic. I'm just saying that what's wrong is the departure point of science, the initial appraisal of what a man is, what the universe is. It's myopic. All the exceptional things humankind has done in the past were done thanks to characteristics that today are catalogued as symptoms and pathologies, like the capacity to become obsessed with a specific thing, a project, an idea, a work of art. I'm just saying that they don't want to cure, but to purify and purge. Instead, they need to know how to tell good, constructive craziness from the evil, destructive kind."

Gianluca nods.

"Oh Mario, how I understand you. I have been divided between those two types of craziness since I was born."

"As for me," says Giorgio, "they didn't let me do fifth grade in primary school, because in class I was either fighting or crying. One day, the teacher told my grandfather, 'Giorgio has to be with children like him.' Like him how? Why, what am I like? I never bothered anyone, but if they bothered me, laughing in my face, sticking out their tongue at me, I got angry. Then the police come, the ambulance comes, everybody blames me, because I'm the lunatic. They're the ones who provoked me, but they get to be the healthy ones, see?"

"Well if they provoke you, you just stick out your tongue too and leave. If you knew the names I got called—retard, faggot—think what I had to put up with. Many of them didn't even know me, and they kicked me in the ass, spat in my face."

Giorgio doesn't answer. His eyes have gone from awake to asleep with the ease and sweetness of a child. Mario is tired, too. He slowly stretches out on the bed and gives me one last look.

"Good night," he says.

"Good night Ma'," I say. I turn to Gianluca.

"Good night Gianlu'," I say.

"Good night Danie'," he replies.

It's the first time I hear people speak my language.

More than the others, Mario seems to be able to read me. Over the years, he has found words to describe things I am not yet able to bring into focus, but that are asking and calling me from inside.

For all their shabby appearance and miserly belongings, maybe these men with whom I share the room and one week of my life, despite all the visible and invisible differences, are the closest to me, to my real nature, that I have ever come across.

DAY 4
FRIDAY

The World Cup starts today. I don't like opening ceremonies. They're almost always clownery: circus spectacles driven by rhetoric. Even more so this time around, when they're hosted by none other than the United States, the most exhibitionist and least soccer-inclined nation on the planet. The first game is not worth watching, either: Germany–Bolivia. Not if my life depended on it.

The good news is that the heat in the room has not increased.

The bad news is that it hasn't let up either.

After the breakfast ritual, Pino got busy changing the sheets. He really had promised to do it yesterday after lunch, but it was all for the best. With all the sweating we did during the night, it would have been for naught. As he labored through the umpteenth bed huffing and cursing, I was about to say something funny to him, more or less like this: "Come, come now, Pino, it can't be that bad." Or: "You're going to have to do my bed over again. It came out terrible." But after his zillionth grunted expletive, I understood that it wasn't a good idea.

After changing six beds, Pino is perspiring at an alarming rate. His white T-shirt is like wet tissue paper on his bulging stomach. As he wipes his face with a roll of paper towels taken from my nightstand without asking for permission, he comes over.

"Hey, listen. What did the harpy have to say?"

The glimmer I see in his eyes leaves no doubt. The closest version to the truth that these ears have heard is Rossana's.

"She asked about you," I say.

Pino jumps like a spring. He grabs me by the arm.

"What did she say to you?" I look at him in all his unappealing state. My words must reconcile truth and kindness.

"What did she say, well, she knows you speak badly about her. She says, though, there's a, shall we say, a precise reason." He stares at me as if I were an exotic animal he'd never seen before.

"What reason?" he asks.

"That when the two of you started working here, you fell in love with her, but she," I make an unambiguous gesture. Already flushed by the sheets he has changed and the suffocating heat, Pino turns blue in the face.

"I liked her? Me? She was the one lusting after me!"

Neither of us believes him.

Not having any more arguments in his defense, Pino opts to flee. He's composed, steps away slowly, but he definitely flees.

Mario and Alessandro are in the room with me. Madonnina is drifting around the corridor, his diaper freshly changed. I don't know the whereabouts of Gianluca and Giorgio, maybe they're watching television.

I go over to Mario and his window. In addition to the pleasure of listening to him, I hope to enjoy a minimal amount of air.

Screams ring out, making both of us jump.

They had never reached such gut-wrenching intensity.

"Those are from the evil ward," I say.

We see Pino striding toward the door that divides us from them. Mario is stunned by the screams. He's a man who is incapable of detaching himself from his surroundings, for better or for worse.

"Do you think they're really evil on the other side? I mean worse off than we are?" I ask.

I've never doubted what the doctors and nurses said, and the shouts and wailing confirmed it day after day.

"Why do you ask? Who is in there, then?" Mario winks at me, "I promised Mancino that I wouldn't say, but you're a clever young man. Now please excuse me." Mario heads for the bathroom.

I remain alone in the room, alone except for Alessandro, still staring at his target above my bed. I go over to him and sit down in the spot where his father usually sits. I just sit there and look at him. Only the blinking of his eyes and his breathing remain alive. It would seem a spell had been cast over him. The affair about the crooked wall that the father tells everybody about, and that he believes is the cause of the illness, in reality could have been just the spark. Alessandro carried the flame inside him, in the shadow of his mind, ready to swallow it. Cautiously I pull back the sheet. There is the arm where every day the father tries to turn him back on, bring him back to life. One area of his forearm is purple. Like stars in the sky, dozens of red welts, pinched bunches of skin, one after another, day in, day out, all equally useless. I do not allow myself to lengthen the list of attempts. But I understand the father's anger, and his questions about this illness so similar to living death. I lean in to his ear.

"Alessandro," I say.

"Alessa'." I follow my words with a gesture—my hand on his shoulder. I shake him. I try to wake him up, break the spell. Perhaps someone new, a face he does not know, can succeed where others have failed.

Like every other attempt until now, mine ends in the emptiness of his eyes.

Gianluca and Giorgio come back into the room looking like two little boys ready for a day's worth of adventures.

"Hey you two! You look like Siamese twins. Joined at the hip," I say.

Giorgio is sipping fruit juice from a straw. He listened to my line without showing any reaction.

"Are you jealous?" he asks.

I take a good look at him, then I understand his question is dead serious.

"No, of course not. I'm glad you two have become friends."

Gianluca has followed the brief exchange with growing enjoyment. Feeling like the object of jealousy makes him absolutely happy. He's thrilled. He plops down on the bed and crosses his legs, brimming with joy.

"Good morning," says an elderly female voice, barging into the room.

Gianluca recomposes himself at once.

A signora, not under seventy-five, stops at the foot of his bed.

"Ciao, Ma'," he greets her.

Gianluca nervously fiddles with his lock of red hair. His mother's hair is puffed with hair-spray, and platinum blond. From her faultless make-up to her red-lacquered nails, she is eager to show how impeccably groomed, how neatly precise she is, despite that everything about her speaks of modest origins and carefully concealed poverty—her clothes, her shoes, her handbag.

The mother stands there stiffly at her son's feet.

"Were you able to make a reputation for yourself here? Did you?"

Gianluca gasps, looks for air with his mouth, looks at us full of shame, humiliated.

"Ma', everybody likes me here. They say my illness is regressing, that after this week of mandatory, I can come home. It's true, ask them yourself. We get along, right?"

As if we were a flock of trained animals, the whole room agrees in unison. Except Alessandro, obviously.

She neither seems reassured nor is she less ferocious than before.

"You still haven't acted like a pig with anyone? Huh?"

Gianluca studies his chewed and painted nails. He's not trying to answer anymore.

The mother turns to us for one second. She stares at us, pausing on the T-shirt worn by Giorgio. She turns back to her son violently.

"Isn't that shirt yours? Did you start giving your things away? Who gave you permission?"

"It's too big for me. He didn't have fresh clothes, so I lent it to him. Right Gio'?"

Giorgio moves his big head affirmatively, but she doesn't look in his direction.

The girl living inside Gianluca is hurting so much that she cries. She's shattered, crushed by the mother's inhuman weight.

"I brought you a change of clothes. Give me your dirty wash so I can go."

Gianluca shoots off the bed. The notion that his public punishment is coming to an end makes him instantly frenetic. He yanks a plastic bag from his locker and hands it to his mother.

"Thanks Ma'." He gives her two kisses on the cheeks. She turns to us and produces a broad smile, incomprehensible after the words she used to pepper her son, with us as the embarrassed witnesses.

"Arrivederci everyone," she says, and heads toward the door with the gait of an elderly woman. She crosses the threshold and disappears.

I have to sit down on the bed. I drink from the bottle—anything to not see Gianluca in emotional distress. The others return to their respective spaces as well.

"That bitch."

He calls for our attention. I try to imagine their past, what determined it, what unhinged it, what were the causes, the faults, the justifications. But it's not about who's right. I know one thing, because I see it, and it's about the present. It's the effect the mother has produced in her son. His face is upset, his tears are mixed with some sort of black make-up. As tough and unjustifiable as it was, no past can tolerate a similar present, handed from mother to son by the crack of a whip.

"For her, it's all part of my illness, all of it. Even the fact that I'm a fag is because I'm ill. Am I allowed to love the person I want? No, because it's my illness. Am I allowed to have hope in something? No, because it's sick to hope. Sick."

Gianluca's eyes are crazed, he's talking to himself now.

I can't take it any longer.

The corridor is infused with Gianluca's mother's perfume. It might be an involuntary clue that makes everything evident, crystal clear. In front of me is the glass door of the bad patients. I've been so stupid. That's why Mario alluded to me being a clever boy, evidently something I was not until a second ago.

I set about looking for Pino. I find him looking out of the window in the television room in the vain attempt to find some fresh air, that faint breeze that sometimes enters. He was hoping no one would see him, but it didn't work. He was smoking a cigarette, and quickly extinguished it on the outside wall next to the window.

"What is it?" he says, continuing to peer outside. He seems melancholy. I might be wrong, but I have the impression that the reason for his mood is rooted back in time, and the reason is called Rossana.

"Now this time you have to tell me the truth. You know me now, I'm a good person, I don't make trouble. There are no evil patients on the other side of that door, are there?" I ask.

"Of course there are, the bad ones are in there. One of them especially is a beast."

I stare at him. My expression makes it more difficult for him to keep up the act. He goes back to looking at the horizon. Today, too, earth and sea are blurred by the imperious mugginess.

"The women are back there, right?"

He does not answer.

"Why the hell did you have to invent that hogwash?"

He shakes his head. The look he gives me is pained.

"This is the billionth demonstration that you don't understand shit about life. Do you know how many times we had to rush to the bathrooms, back when the ward was all open? Do you know how many patients we found humping? Locked into one another? Until one day a girl got pregnant in here, by another loony who then threw himself from the Ariccia bridge. So the head physician invented this thing. Many discover it's a crock of shit, like you, but by then they're just about out of our hair anyway."

Pino wants to continue tearing me down, but he realizes the whole story has not left me indifferent.

"You're young. Try to not end up in here anymore. This place is a circle of torment. Not just for you loonies. Anyone who enters remains imprisoned."

He gives me a pat on the shoulder and goes off down the corridor. Now I stand at the window, alone.

This hangar of illness and desperation, of clear-headed madness, gave birth to a child. A baby conceived inside a circle of torment, to use Pino's words. In the sky whitened by hot humid air, I try to make out the possible features, the profile of what might be a teenager.

A child born of an instable mother and a suicide victim is travelling the world.

A prince.

A Messiah.

A future man capable of anything, that's right, because it's too easy: I cannot allow myself here, now, to imagine him as a misfit, marginalized, true to the blood that begot him.

No.

In him, the sum of bad elements has turned into supreme good, beauty, balance, a future worthy of the name.

I see him among a thousand girls, stronger than all kinds of hateful gossip and all types of prejudice.

Go.

Honor thy father and thy mother.

Prove to all humanity that from the last, from the outcasts, miracles like you are born.

I resist the poignancy, but my view changes rapidly. It darkens the sky. Weeping covers the earth.

Here it is.

Never born.

An error generated by madness. Intolerable. A life that does not deserve to be alive. Because from two sick people can only be born a worse ill.

Sudden tiredness mixes with my tears. The ward is on the second floor, meaning maximum eight meters above ground. I could hang on to the windowsill and the meters would become less. Maybe if I threw myself off properly, I wouldn't even get that hurt.

I hear the electric click of the ward's entrance door, and sound of wheels. It's the lunch cart, wearily dragged by Pino.

I can't decide whether to wear a watch or not. None of us in the room has one. Of course the boredom spelled out by the hands would be exasperatingly excessive at some moments, much like the hours spent at a school-desk. But not knowing precisely what time it is is enervating. You count on the sun, nailed high up in the sky, during infinite days like only summer days can be. In the end, what marks my time is the scant list of activities that can be done in here. Today at least, I await one such activity with justified trepidation.

I'm going to see Cimaroli soon. On my nightstand is the sheet of paper with my poem, folded with meticulous precision. During the session I want to read it to him. The trepidation is soon explained: His judgement, like that of any other living being, interests me much.

When I enter the doctor's office, I am very tense. But first I have to ask about something entirely different.

"You took away the Phenegran. I suffer from insomnia. With the heat and everything else, I have a really hard time." Cimaroli has opened my folder in front of him.

"I'm sorry, but you're at risk. With your disorders, you have an increased probability of developing an addiction. Not just to drugs, but you also have to watch out for sleeping pills and alcohol."

What to answer? He continues.

"I am sorry about yesterday, but I got delayed at the emergency room for four hours. How did it go with Mancino?"

As I usually do with doctors, I try to find conciliatory words, but then I change my mind.

"Bad. To be honest, I don't like him as a doctor. I find him arrogant and uninterested."

Cimaroli stiffens and makes an attempt to soften my words with a smile, but he falters.

"Mancino is a bit rough around the edges, but believe me, he's a good doctor."

Again I do not know what to answer. I wouldn't know how to decipher his embarrassment. Maybe he too thinks I'm just an ignorant cynic, or maybe he is bothered by my calling his colleague's professionalism into question.

"Let's get back to us. I still wanted to ask you about your consumption of drugs. At what age did you start? With what?"

"At age thirteen I got intoxicated when a can of paint

spilled at home. That's when I discovered that certain substances have an effect on the mind. I began, how shall I say, experimenting. I discovered my mother's hair-spray. I'd spray it into the cap and breathe it in. Once they found me half unconscious in the bathroom."

Cimaroli writes everything down meticulously. With inexcusable delay, I interrogate myself about the whole situation. Why am I telling this? Why am I so open about myself? How can I speak so candidly about my habits? Some are even full-fledged felonies. They are going to firebrand me for all the years to come. Pino's face comes to my mind's eye again: I'm twenty years old and don't understand shit about life.

Cimaroli has finished writing. He's looking at me now.

"So what are you going to do with my folder, with the pathology you're going to ascribe to me at the end of my mandatory commitment? Are you going to send it to the Tribunal? What's going to happen after?" I ask.

"Don't worry, we only send a notice of the end of treatment to the Velletri Tribunal. Obviously, if crimes have been committed in here, we communicate that. But we don't mention pathologies and drug consumption. That doesn't mean we throw away what we're doing. We will come to a diagnosis, give you a treatment to follow, let your municipality know about the end of your commitment, and require the healthcare system to take charge of you."

"Meaning?"

"Not much, just that you'll have a social worker."

I find the idea that this treatment is producing effects with a bearing on my future to be extremely upsetting. Social worker? To do what? Why? But Cimaroli does not tap in to what I am thinking.

"The other day we spoke about your mood. Do you ever feel very sad? To the point of having bad thoughts? Of suicide?" he asks.

"I am often very sad, but rarely think of suicide. Except that night I was brought here. Regarding sadness, a strange thing happens to me. I have to think how to explain it properly."

He nods, assuming a waiting posture. Today the doctor is dressed in a Ralph Lauren T-shirt. I recognize the little horse. It's dark blue. His neck is not particularly long, and this type of shirt does not seem to be the best choice for him. Indubitably, a polo jersey would be better.

"It's as if I were split, as if I were two people in one. When I'm with others, I'm the friendly guy, I like to laugh and am able to keep the sadness and the melancholy at bay. But when I'm alone," I pause.

I don't feel like talking anymore. Thinking of the monsters emerging from my solitude has murdered what little of my energy had survived the heat.

"What happens when you are alone?" Cimaroli's pen hangs in mid-air waiting for me to finish the sentence.

"When I'm alone, I get eaten alive."

"Have you ever undertaken psychotherapy treatment?"

"At least three times, but it felt like an act, I don't know why. Somebody talking about themselves seems too easy. You can say or not say whatever you want. Or maybe I'm just not suited."

My tiredness mixed with a sense of profound resignation does not allow me to control my diction. Speaking Italian takes so much effort.

The thought that shortly I will read my poem lifts my spirits. In all, Cimaroli will be the third human being to hear my words.

"How are things with your mother? You mentioned the death of your grandmother and how it was quite a blow to her."

I feel vaguely dazed, like I forgot who I really am and where I'm from.

"Well, my grandmother died in 1984. I was ten. Mamma went through a bad patch. But now . . ." I try.

Cimaroli brings a hand to his wet forehead.

"I apologize, I got you mixed up with another boy, Frascati. You're Mencarelli."

He dives into the written pages, trying to find me there.

"You are," he trails off.

He speed-reads line after line.

"Of course. You do the poetry, right?"

He smiles at me. His eyes go to the folded paper.

"Good, you brought it with you."

Instinctively, I hide the paper behind my back.

"Yes, but I'm still working on it. I'm not sure yet."

"Fine, as you wish."

He doesn't notice I'm lying. He doesn't notice anything, not even my disappointment, my eyes that are unable to conceal the offense. I am not an interesting clinical case for him. Nor was I for Mancino, his colleague. For him, I do not deserve a place in his memory; my name, my surname, my face do not deserve a place. For him I am a lowly mechanism to put back together, a factory-made mechanism, mass-produced, that came off the conveyor belt a bit lopsided.

Everyone is in the room except Giorgio, who had to see Cimaroli after me. I throw the paper on the nightstand and myself on the bed. I hug the pillow. I stay there, clutching nothing. I have an overwhelming desire to leave myself, forget about everything.

"I've lost my soul, Mary! Help me, my little Madonna!"

Not even Madonnina is able to snap me out of it.

"I've lost my soul, Mary! Help me, my little Madonna!"

He's standing up between my bed and his. Pino has put his pajama bottoms back on. Underneath them is the clear protuberance of the diaper. I lift my head toward him.

"What is it Madonni'? What'd you do?"

Silence. The usual staring in the direction of nowhere.

"Mario, what do I do? Call Pino? What do you think he wants?" I ask.

Mario shrugs his shoulders. I turn to Gianluca. He, too shrugs. I rise from the bed. I link arms with Madonnina.

"Want to go for a little walk?"

My question falls into the void, obviously.

When we get to the corridor, I let go of his arm. Madonnina is about as tall as I am, but twenty kilos lighter. His olive complexion, black beard and thinning hair make me think he's from the South. The brownish pajamas he wears—the only article of clothing he has, worn through at the elbows, with the collar threadbare and fraying—are nonetheless of good make and brand. Who knows, maybe Madonnina is from a well-off family. Maybe they're looking for him in some remote area of the South. That's why no one ever comes to visit him. How to track down a person who is unable to reveal his identity in any way?

Or maybe, more probably, there is no wealthy family in the South searching for him. The brand-name, well-made pajamas are just discarded hand-me-downs that happen to have ended up on his back via the charitable act of some do-gooder. I have time to waste. I can fill the hours with hypotheses, but one thing is for certain. No one ever comes to see Madonnina. Why is that? How can there not be one person on the face of this earth with the same blood running through their veins? One. Just one who wishes Madonnina well, who wants to contribute to that, even just one hour per week.

I leave him there in the middle of the hall, closed inside his world.

From their beds, Mario and Gianluca have observed the scene. Now it's my turn to shrug, to show the uselessness of my action, but what else can we do?

I pick up the poem I threw so roughly on the nightstand. I open the sheet of paper and begin reading silently. I like it.

"What's that?"

From his magic enclosure, Mario has seen all. I quickly fold the page up and put it back where it was.

"Nothing. I mean. Sometimes I write. Poems."

"Really?"

Mario has trouble believing me. I nod.

"I read them to my mother. I wanted to read one to Cimaroli, but in the end I chose not to."

"I love poetry, really love it. At school I used to read many poems to my pupils. *'Je est un autre'*."

His last words are in French, at least that's what I think. He looks at me hopefully. I don't know what he expects.

"'I is another.' Don't you know Rimbaud? *Une saison en enfer. A Season in Hell*?"

"I've read Baudelaire, *The Flowers of Evil*, but not yet Rimbaud."

"You must read Rimbaud, absolutely. I'm convinced you'll like him even more. You'll become brothers, I'm sure. What poems do you like? Which ones do you know?"

"I'm not a literature student. I read poetry for my own pleasure. I know Dario Bellezza, Umberto Saba. I like honest poetry. It's the way I like to write, too. If not, my mother wouldn't understand my poems. What I think is that the words need to get to the marrow. You have to strip yourself bare. But many poets seem to dress themselves up. They hide behind their clothes."

"Do you know Giorgio Caproni?"

"No," I say.

"You'd like him, too. My pupils used to really enjoy him because he doesn't jumble things too much. The simplicity of his words is the simplicity of what defines us."

"Thanks."

"Why don't you read what you wrote?"

I feel my face erupting in flames of embarrassment. I brush my hair off my sweaty brow.

"No, I'd rather not."

"Why not?"

Virtuous Mario asks without understanding. I see this, and concede.

"I'm embarrassed."

"In front of us, Danie'?" asks Gianluca, strangely serious. "No one judges anyone in here. If we did, we'd be here for another thirty years."

Despite my tight throat and racing heart, I give it a go.

"All right," I say.

I've never read to more than one person before.

I clear my throat. It's showtime. Like my friends who threw themselves from the Pope's cabin.

You're always the one to pick me up.
My memory is full
of you popping in and carrying me off.
At school I feigned
all kinds of disorders
to see you appear.
Until today, when nothing is feigned
and the illness breaking me is true,
and waiting for you is more atrocious,
having shifted from a desk
to this white cot.

I look at no one, fold up the paper. It was not a good idea to read this poem. The memory of my mother and her absence have sunk me deep into nostalgia for her and my home.

"It's really beautiful."

Mario's eyes shine, his head is slightly slanted to one side. He seems to want to look at me from a different angle.

"Thanks, Daniele," Mario says.

I am so moved I cannot stand still. I scratch my head, I'm sweating; I try to reciprocate their acknowledgements.

"Thank you Ma'," I say.

"You can tell how much you love you mother. Sweet," says Gianluca following suit, with a different type of graveness in his eyes. He seems absorbed in formulating something in his mind. No particular sensitivity is needed to imagine the person stirring all of it up.

"I'm just an amateur, but I think you ought to have someone read it who can help you," says Mario. Without knowing it, he touches upon my biggest concern, a thorn in my side. It makes me jump up from the bed.

"I tried. I just want to know if the stuff I write is worth something. Instead, all I find are sneaks who want to make a quick buck. 'You have talent. Let's publish a book.' Then they want you to give them three million lire to print something that no one is ever going to read. It's called vanity publishing. But that's not for me. A book is a serious thing. It's like scaling a mountain when you've never been up a hill."

Giorgio comes back in from the doctor's office.

"What're you talking about?"

"Poetry," says Gianluca, giving himself a cultured, erudite air. Giorgio looks at him in disgust.

"I don't like it. I like cartoons and dirty magazines."

Everyone laughs.

The memory of my mother is stuck in my throat.

"Hello?"

"It's me," I say.

"Your father told me about your hair."

"It's nothing. It's already growing back. The least of my worries."

"Why, what're you worried about?"

A morass. From now on I will have to weigh my every word in order to not end up being swallowed whole by my mother's anxiety.

"Nothing, nothing. It's just a figure of speech."

"Who's this who lit your hair on fire?"

In her voice I can perfectly hear the warm-blooded animal in her, the female mammal whose pup has been swiped at. She's on the alert and ready to attack in order to defend.

"Enough already. If I tell you it's nothing, it's nothing. Stop worrying."

"But did you tell anyone? Will this person try to do it again?"

"It's a guy who is not well, really unwell. I think he doesn't even realize he did it. He's not nasty. The burned hair is the least painful thing."

"Why, did he do something else to you?"

Now the morass sucks me in up to my waist.

"I'm not talking about physical pain, Mamma."

"Can you please explain better? You're not making any sense."

"What? You still don't understand? I'm talking about the usual. It hurts to even look around in this place. People are suffering more than I thought possible. I have you; they only have their mental disease."

As I speak I see my roommates before me, one by one, their solitude, their social disadvantage, years and years spent battling their disorder, often against the very people who came running to help them, who are worse than the malady itself.

All these things I knew from hearsay.

"That's why you need this experience. You're twenty, still a boy. You have your whole life ahead of you."

"Yes, I know."

To be able to change. I'd like that.

But I cannot replace my eyes, cannot prevent my nature

from running its course. Who can take away the suffering? What task must I complete to no longer feel the pain of others? Will maturity, becoming an adult, toughen my skin? I can only hope so. Although if I look at my roommates, some are much older than I, so my preoccupation prevails. By no means has time given them a carapace.

"We'll talk tomorrow. Take care of yourself," my mother says.

"Say hi to Papa," I answer.

The opening ceremony of the American World Cup is first-class buffoonery, worse than I had imagined. Hordes of men and women squeezed into improbable costumes. Diana Ross is forced to run and sing at the same time, then perform some kind of penalty kick in order to breathe life into a farce not even Benny Hill could have staged. Mamma mia.

Unlike many of my friends, I do not have a manifest aversion toward the United States, but it's political for them, no matter if they're on the left or the right. Ideology, with its presumption of a static reality, with all its unshakable certainties, is the farthest thing from my nature. I say this with good reason, from first-hand experience, and my story, the things I have done until now, confirm it.

I am twenty. At seventeen, I declared war on life. It all began with a trip, a trip homeward from Misano Adriatico, on foot through half of Italy, alone and without a penny to my name.

I brought a thousand possible solutions to bear on my dissatisfaction. I refused to close the door on any experience, however extravagant. I looked for myself everywhere. In political parties, churches, and places of all kinds of depravity. I tried to open invisible doors with the help of every drug, legal and illegal.

There were moments of gratification, but then everything vanished, and I went after it in hot pursuit.

On this unbridled race I find myself performing, running on the heels of an unknown and probably nonexistent prey, I have come across men nailed to their version of the facts.

I have known old men living in a past that was dead and gone. They were there with their black-and-white photos of Mussolini kept in their wallets like relics to honor by weeping, offered to a stranger's eyes as the solution to all evil, to this country, to the entire world.

I have also seen many people my age living in a past that was dead and gone. They idolized warriors drawn on the walls of community centers; they venerated economic theories as if they were sacred scriptures; they blindly believed that everything would change if only there was enough hatred of power and those who represented it. Anarchy was the final solution.

I believed everything, then I refuted it.

I wounded myself with all the life I could muster to arrive here and now with one single certainty to defend.

Everything I have been through, whether it's a lot or a little, is not the prey I am looking for.

The ceremony continues in spectacular fashion, one firework after the other, but I've finished my cookies, which is the real reason I have come to the television room. In the bedroom, the odor of the hospital dinner was unbearable, so strong as to prevent me from eating with proper appetite. The dish that was guilty of its own smell was grilled chicken breast, seemingly innocuous, accompanied by boiled zucchini.

According to the forecast, today is going to be the last day of the record-breaking heatwave. I really hope so. Like background music, barely perceptible, rancidity is starting to waft up again in the room. Same old song, a broken record.

As she clears away the remains of dinner, Rossana looks especially tired, and her shift has just begun.

"Everything okay?" She was not expecting my question.

"That's overstating it," she answers vaguely. But the need to talk is something everyone feels, both the healthy and the loony.

"I spent four hours in line at the social security office today. My husband's disability has to be reviewed every two years. Reviewed? Maybe Christ will come along and make him better. Every two years they have to review everything. It's going to be a while before he's considered permanently disabled."

"They only push you when you're going downhill," I dust off an old adage I've heard from my mother and father thousands of times when there's nothing else to say to your interlocutor, when common sense is nixed by the enemy of the day.

She closes the conversation with a smile, a portrait of ruefulness.

"How do I look?"

Gianluca addresses Giorgio and me. He is wearing a kind of garishly colored scarf he has turned into a tank top, knotted behind his neck, very tight around his belly and chest.

"Nice!" Giorgio answers first. I consider the question answered, but Gianluca insists on my opinion by pointing at me with his chin.

"You look good, but aren't you hot all wrapped up like that?"

Gianluca looks at me with motherly indulgence.

"Hot? This is a scarf! It's like a feather, thin and light. I put it on precisely to cool off."

"Hey, you know what I'd do if I were outside?" Giorgio demands an answer.

"What would you do?"

"I'd have a black-cherry popsicle. Nice and cold."

His invitation to fantasy, to desire, does not deserve to be ignored. I sit up and lean my back against the headboard.

"If I were outside, I'd go to a bar and have me a nice cold

beer. Then around midnight, I'd have an ice cream cone. Now that's the life," I say.

Gianluca feels challenged. He gets out of bed, and looks at us with mock pity.

"Cherry popsicle, ice cream cone, how sad. I'd go strutting around downtown Rome, then go dancing at the Alibi in search of the man of my life."

"Gianlu', we were talking about things to cool us off. You have to go and screw everything up."

"That's right Danie', I like screwing around, and I like being screwed even more." His quip makes him laugh harder than everyone else.

"Instead we're all here inside this oven without a popsicle in sight," says Giorgio, unbelievably lucid. He has found the best words to dampen our zest.

"Psst." It's Mario. He has been absent from our chat until now. He looks at us one by one, inviting us to his corner. I imagine he wants to show us something related to his bird friend, but he stretches his arm out toward the horizon, motioning for us to look in that direction.

The sun is low now, weary after dominating for hours. The boiling air carries the colors of the sunset, lighting up everything with red and orange. There is not a shred of matter before us that is not conquered by the end of this fiery day.

Hovering out there between the sky and the sea, which is also radiant with the setting sun, lies an enormous cruise liner. Despite the haze, it is perfectly visible thanks to the shining lights that follow its contours and decorate it. Strings of bulbs hang from the bridge to bow and stern. More of them, horizontal ones, mark the different levels of the cabins. It is one giant nativity scene, sailing into the sun that is about to sink beneath the line of the sea.

"Listen." Mario cups his ear, urging us to do the same. "In the dining room, the commander is about to take the floor. His moustache is long and flowing, his eyebrows white and bushy. The room is packed. Here he is, 'It is an honor for me to host three celebrities of renown on my ship. This triad of excellencies is known the world over. Let's give them a hand.' Can you hear the clapping?" Gianluca, Giorgio and I look at one another. We hesitate, undecided whether to go along with Mario and his daydream or not. In the end, we nod.

"The commander raises his arm to end the applause. 'Ladies and gentlemen, a moment of your attention please. Allow me to introduce our guests of honor one by one. The first, a talented fashion designer adored by the international jet-set, the woman aspired to by half the world's men, the diva of divas, Gianlucaaa!'"

Called into play, Gianluca overcomes his initial uncertainty. He takes a bow, then begins waving to the many members of the public who have gathered in the dining hall, including the ship's sailors, piled on top of one another just to see her. Gianluca concludes his thanks with a series of kisses blown from the palm of his hand, destined to reach the most distant tables.

"'Let me now introduce a man with superhuman strength, a Titan able to bend steel, a heroic savior of children, our weapon against the evil people of the world. Yes, you guessed it, it's Giorgiooo!'" Giorgio, embarrassment in every corner of his face, an emotional giant, greets the delirious crowd. A love-struck damsel tries to embrace him. He blows kisses to everybody, pats children on the head, raises his formidable arms to the sky in a gesture of victory. The ship's commander attempts to quieten the excitement. He turns toward me.

"'And finally, the man with the soles of wind, the poet who will sing of this voyage and a thousand other adventures, the minstrel of every heartbreak and bliss that his big heart will offer him. Yes, it's him, Danieleee!'" It's difficult to hold in my joy. I bow deeply. "Thank you," I repeat to infinity, once for each member of the hundred-strong audience, on its feet only for me. I look at the ship's commander. The moment has come to act out our gratitude. I have trouble calming the hyped-up throng.

"I believe it is our due to thank the commander of this ship, Mario, the man who has steered us toward the sun, always with a smile on his lips, ready to dole out wisdom with the modesty worthy of the very best. May he receive your warmest applause!" Mario was not expecting this switching of roles. He flourishes the sharpest military salute these eyes have ever seen. The room erupts in jubilation.

"Danie'? Danie', are you awake?"

It's Giorgio, right when sleep was coming my way. All the others are asleep.

"Yes, I'm awake. What is it?"

"I don't know, maybe it's that story with the ship and all, but," he goes mute. Around us is the deep, peaceful breathing of sleeping roommates.

"Come on Gio', tell me what's wrong," I say.

"I have nightmares."

"So what am I supposed to do?"

"Could you hold my hand?" he asks.

I turn on the light above my bed. I look at him in the hope that it's an after-hour joke.

"What are you saying?"

"Come on, could you hold my hand? It won't take me long to fall asleep."

"But we're too far apart, see?"

As a reply, he gets up, grabs my nightstand, effortlessly lifts it out of the way, then shoves his bed against mine.

"There," he says.

Beds and hands are linked.

"We're so ugly when we're dead," says Giorgio.

I see his profile cut out against the room's semi-darkness, lost in who knows what train of thought. Maybe the nightmare that woke him. I give his hand a squeeze and bring it close to my side.

"Let's sleep now," I say.

Giorgio turns toward me. I can see his smile despite the dark.

"Good night, Danie'," he says.

DAY 5
SATURDAY

The lower temperatures they forecasted remained that: a forecast. Waking up is hellacious. Drowsiness mixed with heat. The collar of my T-shirt is soaked with sweat and chafes my skin.

At the foot of my bed stands an intruder clothed in white.

"Do you mind telling me what the hell went on in here last night?"

He's alluding to the beds—Giorgio's and mine—no more than thirty centimeters apart. Luckily he didn't see us holding hands.

"Nothing went on. Giorgio was having nightmares, so he pushed his bed over to mine, that's all," I say.

The nurse lets the information sink in. While Pino is overweight, this one's skinny and gangly. Up and down his puny arms, a labyrinth of greenish veins stands out thickly. Had he not been wearing a uniform, I would have definitely mistaken him for a patient.

"Whatever you say. Now just put the beds back in place, and the nightstand too," says the nurse.

"Isn't Pino here this morning?" I ask.

"Yeah right, as if he'd be in on a Saturday. Here in the psychiatric ward the rules are different from the rest of the hospital. Fixed shifts Monday through Friday. Weekends by rotation, for auxiliaries like me who don't have an assigned ward. Us vagabonds, so to say," explains the nurse.

"So Rossana and Lorenzo won't be here either," I conclude. He nods.

"Theoretically no, but if they want to work an overtime shift, you might find them here, especially tomorrow, 'cause it's Sunday. It's extra money on the ol' pay check."

The nurse considers the conversation ended, but I wasn't through yet.

"Sorry, what's your name? It seems rude not to call you by your name."

"Alberto," he announces, briskly commencing breakfast duty.

Giorgio continues sleeping, oblivious to my dialogue with the nurse, the brightening of the light of day, and the stealthily increasing heat. Shower noises drift in from the bathroom accompanied by Gianluca's gracious singing. He's busy with a Michael Jackson number if I'm not mistaken.

Madonnina's slumber has not been disturbed either—he's lying in a sea of sweat—while Alessandro has not shifted his gaze by one millimeter.

My silent roll-call ends with Mario. As on the other mornings, his routine unfolds slowly, seemingly weighted down by unfathomable thoughts. Undisguised affliction marks his mien as he neatens his nightstand to a T. Everything must be placed with absolute precision—the boxes of medicine, the napkin, the cutlery.

"Good morning Mario," I say.

The smile with which he reciprocates is laden with resignation.

"Everything good?" I ask.

By way of answer, he goes back to tidying his nightstand.

I get up and go over. From the open window comes no air at all. The bird's nest is empty. Perhaps it was so hot that the bird decided to ascend higher, to the Roman Castles, Monte Cavo.

From close up, I'm able to observe what for all intents and purposes can be called a ritual, with Mario's gestures following a preordained scheme. He notices me watching.

"For what it's worth, I try to make things as neat as I can. I cannot suffer disorder. There's too much of it inside me to have to look at it on the outside too," he says.

Being so close, I notice his hands are trembling and his eyes are feverish.

"Everything okay, Mario?" I ask.

The look in his eyes speaks more than any answer.

"Not entirely okay, no. The usual, let's say. Been this way for years and years. I put up with it, nothing more. Some days, what matters is reaching nightfall alive."

I try to find the words for an answer, but fail. Once his rite dedicated to arrangement is finished, he sits down on the bed and motions for me to join him.

"I am devoured by fear. One of my greatest fears takes hold of me at night. I am afraid that madness will take me in my sleep. You know that can happen, right?" he asks.

"I've never heard that," I say.

"The nights are terrible. I'm forced to go through the same nightmares. I know they're coming back again. To infinity. Sooner or later I'll wake up and won't be able to put things in order anymore." Mario begins to weep. He hadn't done that in front of me before. I wring my hands, think of something I can do or say, but remain mute, glued in place.

"The fear of going insane is worse than being insane," he cries.

Mario is probably three times my age, and his ideas are likely backed up by a thousand more memories than I have, but I know the fear he is talking about. I too have experienced the limit when all reality loses meaning, when all reality crumbles and dematerializes before your very eyes—the evening that brought me here, for instance. We sit there, each contemplating our personal vision of insanity. Mario snaps out of it first. He pulls me away almost violently from the thoughts flowing through my mind.

"Do not be seduced by fear. Think of fire. If you look at it too long, if you go too close, it'll burn you," Mario says.

He tries to cheer me up with a smile.

"Yesterday evening and during the night, I thought of your poem. And I thought of poets. I believe artists have one thing in common with psychos: No one can tell them what to look at or how to see it. Call it freedom if you like. In the same way, nothing and nobody can ease their pain. I have a theory about this."

A sort of embarrassment comes over Mario. Usually so convinced of his words and his crystal-clear reasoning, he falters now.

"It's a big thing to say to a mere boy. I believe that artists and certain deranged individuals carry inside them the seed of a very distant memory, something that happened way before all other stories: Beauty, the spark of everything. What I think is that certain people still have a grainy picture of this in their subconscious. These people see everything the way it really used to be, before the thing happened that changed everything."

I try but fail to understand. Mario struggles and seems to not want to continue.

"Why, what happened? You're the one who told me it's useless to judge, so don't worry," I say.

"Some people—they could be blessed; they could be cursed—see beauty in its original state. I'm talking about paradise, because this was paradise. But we sinned, so then death arrived, and time arrived. These people don't know it, but the nostalgia they feel when looking at beauty is the nostalgia for what used to be, for paradise, for God," says Mario.

He goes back to breathing, and now I am the one to have suddenly lost the desire to speak, to do anything at all. He picks up on this and delicately takes me by the shoulder.

"Mine are just the rantings of an elementary school teacher

placed on leave. But keep one thing in mind: Take care of yourself. Ask for help when you need it. Above all, let your mind wander free. Don't let anyone tell you how the world works."

I nod. Standing before Mario, my twenty years are halved, and I see myself as a ten year-old, facing an enormous mountain to climb. Every time, his words touch parts of me that I did not know existed.

To bring paradise on earth into it, original sin. What can I say? After all, aren't I the one who wants everything to have meaning? Could this be the root, planted so deep that I feel it without being able to see it? Because I cannot deny it: I feel that nostalgia. I experience it, just as I experience the incapacity to accept the passing of time. It feels artificial compared to everything that wants to live forever in my heart.

I am like a swimmer suspended in the middle of an oceanic trench. Me, a speck of life without a haven. Below me, kilometers of icy black water ready to embrace me forever.

In the hallway, my vain attempt to detach myself from Mario's considerations brings me face to face with a man in a white coat. He's short, stocky and as tanned as a lifeguard at the end of the season. Alberto the vagabond nurse stands next to him, a stack of medical charts in his hand.

"Go to your bed immediately. The head physician will be making his rounds shortly."

This means that the bronzed, vertically challenged doctor is the head physician.

Back in the room, I share the announcement with the others. We suddenly seem like a group of children on a school trip, trying to tidy the room before the teachers arrive. Giorgio is the busiest. First he puts my nightstand back, then he removes from his bed the dirty socks and undershirt he was wearing when he entered the hospital. They had been left to molder at the foot of the mattress. Like a good housewife, Gianluca is folding items of clothing he had draped on a chair. Then he places them neatly in his locker.

"I've lost my soul, Mary! Help me, my little Madonna!"

Possibly infected by the sudden frenzy, Madonnina does nothing beyond repeating his invocation. I take it upon myself to put him to bed.

Preceded by the nurse, voilà the head physician.

Each patient's medical chart is handed to him by the faithful squire. He gives it a quick glance, then signs it with his pen, a Montblanc of course.

Not a word is uttered. Not a facial expression is seen.

At Mario's bed, however, the head physician raises his eyes.

"How's it going?" Finally, his voice: neutral, colorless.

"Same as ever. No better, no worse," answers Mario with natural affability. The doctor pauses to study him.

"It's been a long time since we last saw each other. You look better. I might be mistaken, but you look calmer and you've put on a bit of weight. Have you decided to eat properly? Living on baked apples alone is not much fun, is it?"

Mario smiles. He seems flattered by so much attention.

"Baked apples are the thing for me. They're all I need."

Neither convinced nor pleased, the head physician nods.

"As you wish. On weekdays, I'm in my office for visits, but if you want to talk or ask me something, tell the nurses and I'll come up."

"Thank you professor, I'll do that."

The head physician and the nurse exit the room.

"Gee whiz Mario, did the two of you do your first communion together, or what? He was so nice to you. Didn't say a word to any of us," sputters Gianluca, quick to feel jealous.

"We've known each other for many years. He's the doctor I had when I was first hospitalized here. You were still a child," says Mario.

Meantime, an intense stench of burning starts wafting in from the window.

"Can you smell that stink?" asks Giorgio. Mario looks out. I go over.

Not too far off, we see an enormous blaze in the middle of the fields at the foot of the Roman Castles.

"There's a fire in the distance," I answer.

If at all possible, the air outside is even hotter than inside. I remain transfixed by the flames whirling up in the sky higher and higher. I'm hypnotized by their voracious, insatiable dance. The heat snaps me out of it. The sun is at its apex, searing the top of my head.

Tonight the national team will be playing its first championship game—against Ireland. In addition, it's Saturday night. Irrepressible bitterness accompanies this fifth day of mandatory treatment.

Scene after scene comes to life on the white walls of the corridor. I see my friends in full line-up, without me, obviously, ready to enjoy the evening and the game. They're having a great time. Then they all head for Rome or the seashore to finish the night that has only just begun.

But here I am, alone, without being able to savor the anticipation, without the shadow of an idea as to what I could do to pass the time.

The whimpering in the hall stops at the door separating us from the nasty patients, that is, the women. It's open. Maybe Alberto left it open during his rounds with the head physician.

I push the door open. The corridor is identical to ours, only that the photos on the walls are different. We have ones of the Roman Castles. They have four views of Rome. The Imperial Fora and the Colosseum on one wall, and the Pantheon and the Baths of Caracalla on the other. Like the corridor, also the layout of the rooms is identical to ours.

Not a single sound in the air. No sign of life.

Noiselessly, a black-clothed figure slips out of one of the patients' rooms. Very long jet-black hair. My curiosity will not be outdone by fear. I close the door, leaving it open a crack.

It's a young woman. Robust physique, wide hips. She doesn't notice me watching her.

One smattering of her face at a time, I recognize her. Middle or maybe elementary school, or perhaps from one of the many groups I became a member of and then left. She might be from Pavona or Albano. She seems to have come out to the corridor for the same reason I did, to idle away the time, to distract her thoughts. She looks like the tranquil type of nutcase, like me— unlike, say, Madonnina.

I open the door wider, centimeter by centimeter. Now my entire face is visible.

She sees me.

Through her eyes, I see the same surprise I have felt when I glimpse a face I know. Her astonishment is greater than mine, maybe because she has not yet discovered that the supposed nasties on the other side of the ward are nothing but a lie. She gives me an imperceptible sign of greeting. I immediately signal back.

Step after step, she comes closer.

She could be my age, but time hasn't been kind to her. She looks much older, more like thirty or thirty-five.

"What are you doing here?" As much as possible, I want my tone to be light and airy. She shrugs, doesn't answer. Meanwhile I review my life in a fruitless attempt to place her in the location where we were once side by side.

"Sorry, it's probably because of this place, but I can't remember where we met," I say in the end, not having other avenues.

She does not hide her disappointment.

"At the church youth club in Pavona. I'm Valentina. Remember?"

Words have the power to slip into your memory and pull out the right pictures. The first times I started going out, barely fourteen years old—it was one adventure after the other.

"Of course! We were just kids."

She smiles. She sidles over.

"Yes. Do you remember this?"

She dangles her right hand, fat and dark, in front of my eyes.

Covered by the flesh of her ring finger, is a ring, impossible to remove.

I look at it for a long while, trying to attribute a meaning, anything, to it, but nothing comes to mind.

It is not valuable. Instead of gems it has pieces of plastic, the sort of bauble you'd find in a pack of chips.

"This is my wedding ring from Francesco. But he disappeared."

A hammer nails a vision to my mind's eye. All becomes clear, flesh and blood.

A summer afternoon like this one. A dirt soccer field. A chorus of cicadas. But above all, our blossoming desire as boys. Our hunger, our fiery staring at the girls, their bodies we dreamed of but had never laid a finger on. Francesco was the eldest, he might have been sixteen. He went around on a tricked-out Vespa.

"He made love to me, three times. I don't know what happened to him after that. I waited for him a long time. In the end I told Mama and Papa. They shouted at me, 'Whore, you whore!' I started smacking my head against the wall and eating cardboard. But Francesco still has to come back. I never took off his ring. Look how pretty it is."

A sense of vertigo, the veins in my wrists are throbbing, going bonkers. I want this to be just a horrid nightmare.

Valentina does not know, but the youth standing in front of

her now, the one trying to hide his pain by looking elsewhere, precisely he is one of the people responsible, an accomplice to her mental illness, to her entire life.

I perfectly remember the preparations. Francesco told us his sights were set on her. We were to make sure her girlfriends heard how madly in love with her he was. We worked on the plan assiduously. It took weeks for her to fall into the trap. I remember the aftermath just as perfectly. The laughter, the stories, Francesco telling anyone with ears how he "had poked her first."

"How many years ago was that? Six, seven? Why don't you forget about it? Find yourself another boyfriend. Why don't you do that?" I am aware of the stupidity of my words, as stupid as they are logical. If only it were that easy. But it's not me speaking. It's my regretful conscience, the desperate wish to somehow finish what has been started.

"I love only him." Her eyes are those of a wild, insensate beast, with the same bottomless pit of black fire that I glimpsed in Madonnina's eyes.

"What the hell are you two doing?"

Alberto runs toward us from the entrance. He violently slams shut the door through which we were talking. No possibility for us to say goodbye.

"Don't worry, nothing happened," I say.

He tries to be ferocious, but you can tell he couldn't care less about us or the ward. Alberto doesn't know how infinitely grateful I am to him for having ended my encounter.

As I head toward my room, I repeat to myself that it was only an adolescent gag, a trick played without malice, similar to many others I heard about and participated in during those years. How could we imagine that such mischief would unleash this kind of insanity?

I do not enter my room, but remain in the hall staring at the wall that's ten centimeters from my nose. In reality, I'm staring at myself.

I am able to do things that hurt people.

Acts that have passed through my life anonymously, unworthy of being committed to memory, have produced pain in the life of others.

Acts that are still being atoned for.

How much have I been stained by cruelty? However stupid, indolent and small it seemed, in truth it's gigantic, like the cruelty I dumped on Valentina. Without succeeding, I try to remember the others who took part in the trick we played on her. Many of them will never know that a prank we pulled one long-ago summer put an end to the happiness of another human being.

I ask for forgiveness. For my entire past, for the present, for what will come.

But whom do I ask it of? I am unable to forgive myself. I just can't.

I punch the wall, just once. The blow echoes through the ward.

It's the magnitude of the remorse that wants to be hurled against something of equal magnitude. Anger and more anger.

The wounds on my knuckles that had almost healed start to bleed again.

Alberto sticks his head out of the dispensary. Gianluca and then Giorgio stick their heads out of the room.

"That thump came from the other side," I say.

No one believes me.

Something good has come from this mandatory committal. Not for my mental health, for sure. But I think I've lost a few kilos. In the bathroom I look at my face, concealed under a one-week beard. I look thinner. Not that it's difficult to explain. I skipped lunch again today. After seeing Valentina I lost my appetite. I don't feel like doing anything. I looked for Mario's eyes, hoping he would intuit my state of mind, but he was busy with his birdie, smiling at it, whispering things.

In place of Alberto the beanpole, there is now a female nurse. She too is auxiliary staff. She's rude. I wasn't even able to ask her name. She's been closed up in the dispensary since she arrived. Maybe she's napping, or maybe she locked herself in there because she's terrified. She has surrendered to the fate that gifted her with a shift in the loony ward. Plus, there's all this heat. It is known that heat and insanity do not mix well. Or maybe they go together just dandy.

I come out of the bathroom and begin breathing again. This week, thanks to the endless variety of stenches, I have trained to hold my breath, just in case I want to take up spear-fishing again, one of the many sports I started and quit. I can go at least a minute and a half without air.

Finally the nurse looks in. I walk over to her. I get the impression that she shrinks back in fright. She instinctively puts her hands on her stomach.

"What is it?" Her voice confirms my impression.

"I wanted to know at what time I'll be seeing Cimaroli," I say. I have a fundamental need to talk to someone who can give me what I am unable to give myself, a bit of indulgence.

"Stay here," she says, going back to the dispensary. I hear her voice resound in the room on the telephone. She comes out.

"On Saturdays and Sundays there are no sessions. But tomorrow afternoon, Cimaroli is on duty."

I take note of this information with regret.

"Thanks. What's your name?"

"Alessia." I take a better, closer look. The nurse is a corpulent young woman with arms bigger than mine, but her belly has a particular roundness to it and she keeps running her hands over it.

"Are you pregnant?"

This possibly frightens her even more.

"Yes, almost five months." She sounds defenseless.

"How nice. Do you know if it's a boy or a girl?"

"Boy."

"Call him Daniele, like me."

She smiles.

"Matteo."

I remain in the corridor imagining the life growing inside Alessia's belly. It's liquid, it sparkles. A fish-man tied to its mother, feeding through her, breathing her air. The flesh we carry is our mother's. My face, heart, hands are all cells I borrowed from her.

"It's me," I say.

"How do you feel? When are they letting you out?"

"If all goes well, I'll be out on Monday."

"What happened? Why do you sound like that?"

I knew my mother would instantly notice my prostration. It's why I called her.

"I bumped into a girl here in the psychiatric ward. I used to know her."

"How come she's in there?"

"That's the point."

"What do you have to do with it?"

Thanks to her powers, our conversation skips the useless chit-chat.

"I do and do not have anything to do with it. Years ago, she went out with a guy who had no serious intentions. He just wanted to have fun. She took it bad. Drove her crazy. See?"

"And where do you fit in?"

"I knew he just wanted to have fun, but I told her girlfriends that he was in love with her. It was a trick to get her to fall for the plan."

My mother crucifies me with her silence. I can see her biting her lip out of disappointment and agitation.

"Ma? Are you there?" I ask.

"Bravo, that was really nice of you. Yet you do have a sister. What if they had done that to her? If you called me because you thought I'd ease your conscience, you're wrong. Of all the bad things we do, those we do in jest, with thoughtlessness, are the absolute worst."

My collapse is vertical. I cry furiously, heaving with increasingly powerful blasts.

"I'm so sorry."

I do not know what else to say. I hear her breathing at the other end.

"Being human doesn't mean scaling mountains, but knowing that every gesture you make has a value, be it good or bad."

I try to stop the tears. I order them to stop, but it is totally futile. We remain as we are, me chewing my grief, she in silence.

"Do you want me to come? I'll stay with you for a bit," my mother proposes.

Her love has returned, the love that makes the sun come up in the morning, that commands the tides with precision.

"No, Ma. It won't be long now. I'll see you at home."

"Now you focus on getting better. Try to eat. If you can't take care of yourself, you won't be able to take care of anyone else."

In the television room, I sit in front of the black screen trying to get Valentina's face out of my mind. I imagine her on the other side of the wall, lying on her bed, busy admiring the ring embedded in her finger. Like every other wretched nutcase in here, she is nailed to her past, to the spark that caused everything to explode.

Coldly I tell myself that Valentina is no different from Alessandro and so many others. His mental disorder arrived with a partition under construction, hers with a boy's deception and his false declaration of love. But this does not lighten the burden of my responsibility, as a hideous lackey, a fool, by one gram. I understand there is only one judge that will be able to pardon me: time. No one else can do it because I don't deserve it. I promise myself I'll try to look up Valentina's family once I'm out of here. I'll tell them the truth about what happened so many years ago. This will not restore her mental health, but the parents need to know; they must take back their insults, for she was not a whore, just a girl like many. If anything, she is at fault for having fallen in love with the wrong guy. She's the victim of an offense inflicted light-heartedly, making it even more inexcusable.

I decide to take a shower. The last few hours have left their mark. I am sticky and greasy. I need to clean myself up and see myself as different from how I see myself now. Even if taking a shower in the hospital room's bathroom is not as enjoyable as it is at home.

I open the door.

It takes me a few seconds to comprehend.

Giorgio is in front of me.

Kneeling in front of him is Gianluca.

I immediately close the door.

I suspect my shower just got postponed.

Mechanically, I go to my locker. I start reorganizing my jeans, my T-shirt. Not that it's really necessary.

After a while they come out of the bathroom.

With an extremely relaxed air, Giorgio gives me a smack on the shoulder, throws himself on the bed, does not seem embarrassed in the slightest, and sets about staring at the ceiling with dreamy eyes.

Without looking at me once, Gianluca heads toward his corner, sits down, crosses his bony legs, and starts caressing his mottled red hair. Unlike Giorgio, he seems troubled.

Silence.

Given my Valentina episode, I cannot afford more discomfort, fighting or incomprehension. At this moment, I need other human beings, even loony ones, to take me into their midst and open up to me with words and smiles.

"Italy's playing tonight," I say.

Gianluca pounces on my offering of normalcy.

"That's right! Let's watch the game together!"

I nod. He hops off the bed, the girl inside him is jumping with joy.

"I want to watch with you, too," says Giorgio, inviting himself to the party.

"This is the life! What more could we want?" exclaims Gianluca. He's so excited he can't keep still. I want to say that there is actually quite a bit more we could want from life, but I join in his cheer instead. Right now, it's like water in the desert.

"Nothing, that's what. Couldn't ask for better," I say.

The idea comes to me in front of yet another bowl of broth. I see on the face of my roommates—and here I refer to the clear-headed ones, those who do not subsist on baked apples alone: Giorgio and Gianluca—the same disappointment as they contemplate the tepid slop. And resorting to the pocket of cookies has tired me, nauseated me.

"I have an idea," I say.

I ring the bell.

I hope what I have in mind is possible. Alessia looks out of the medical dispensary. I'm taken aback.

"How come you're still here? Isn't the afternoon shift over yet?" I ask.

"I'm doing afternoon and night. Then I'm off tomorrow and the day after. Nights are worth gold. Why did you call?"

All eyes converge on me.

"I have a request. Over the past week, they've intoxicated

us with soups. Plus, there's the game tonight. Would it be possible to order a pizza? Maybe somebody else here would like one, too."

Like flowers in the morning sun, the faces of Giorgio, then Gianluca, and even Alessia open up into unadulterated smiles, expressions of ecstasy mixed with irrepressible hunger follow.

"I don't know if it's allowed," she says. But she definitely wants a pizza.

"Please," begs Gianluca, joining his hands in a fervent, theatrical plea. Giorgio immediately does the same.

"What harm is there? There's no rule against psychiatric patients ordering out a pizza," I say.

Alessia ponders my words.

"True, it isn't written anywhere that you cannot have a pizza delivered," she muses.

Now is supposed to be the easy part, but there are always hitches on the way from theory to practice. The most important:

"Any of you have cash?"

Giorgio and Gianluca exchange surprised glances of perplexity.

"I have four, maximum five thousand lire," says Gianluca.

"All I have is five hundred lire in change," replies Giorgio.

Of the pair, Gianluca is Mr. Moneybags.

I take twenty thousand lire from my cabinet. My mother had put them in the sack for me, for emergencies.

"I have this. Along with yours, it should be enough," I say, waving the banknotes in the air. Giorgio and Gianluca erupt in agitated, excited yelps. They rush over to hug and kiss me.

"If you end up being a few thousand short, I'll chip in," says the famished Alessia, closing the discussion. She's as happy as us crazies.

Two margherita pizzas for Alessia and Gianluca, one

capricciosa for Giorgio, and a four-cheeses for me. There's even some money left for fried rice balls.

We unsuccessfully attempt to involve Mario in the extraordinary dinner. He really does not want to. But he does enjoy seeing us so happy. Especially when the pizzas are delivered to the room, we jump for joy like little kids.

The most voracious is Alessia. She polishes off the pizza and rice ball in five minutes at most. She was twice as hungry, no exageration. Giorgio was pretty quick wolfing it down, too. The slowest are Gianluca and I. He eats his like a queen mother, with fork and knife, while I impose the slow pace on myself in order to get the most out of every bite.

Because of the time difference, the game starts after ten. Alessia breaks up the pizza boxes into a heap of little shreds, then dumps them into containers for special waste so that no one will ever find a trace of our supper. She cleans up and says goodnight. We reply with two goodnights—one for her and one for little Matteo.

Italy gets off to a poor start. The team seems tense, off their game.

Barely ten minutes later, we go under, 1–0. It's too easy to blame Gianluca Pagliuca; the real mistake belongs to Franco Baresi. We are unable to react. Now the Irish believe in a second goal.

The game progresses without a frisson. Plus, Giorgio and Gianluca are not huge soccer enthusiasts. It's definitely not the same as watching with my friends or with my father and brother.

The triple whistle clobbers us with defeat. Arrigo Sacchi's game is below par for a national team. His many detractors were right.

Disappointed, especially me, we go back to our room. But it was a nice evening—we had good food and we felt free.

"How'd it end?"

Mario is still up, wondering what the score was. He understands by looking at our faces.

"How much?"

"One to zero." He's sorry like us. He comes over with small steps. Except for when he heads to the bathroom, I've rarely seen him leave his corner.

"Can I ask you a favor?"

"Of course," I say.

Mario makes a sign of thanks. He looks timid.

"Would you mind giving me a cookie? I'd like to give it to the sparrow, just a few crumbs at a time. I'm afraid it's having trouble finding food in this heat."

I reach for the roll of cookies and hand him a couple.

"Tell me if you need more."

The gratitude Mario shows is something that all existing human beings should see at least once in their life. Like an artistic masterpiece, or a wonder of nature.

The game ended a bit past midnight. After roughly half an hour of casual indignation and chatter, all my roommates drift off to sleep. Only one remains awake—me.

The image of Valentina is impressed on the inside of my eyelids.

Even the fun I just shared with my companions has given way to suffering, though I can't say that's anything out of the ordinary; even when I'm at home or with my friends I experience this transformation. From joy to melancholy and sadness. What makes me suffer is the idea that the life we live ends up in nothingness, that there is no way to experience it again, to see everybody again.

"I've lost my soul, Mary! Help me, my little Madonna!"

It makes me jump, like always.

Madonnina is lying on his bed. Despite the fact that the heat has not let up by one degree, he is shaking with cold, at least that's what I think the reason is. I take the sheet and cover him up to his neck.

He looks at me with his mournful eyes steeped in a perennial night, like Valentina's.

"Sleep, Madonni.'"

Alessandro's face slathered in white foam is the first thing I see in the morning. His father sits in his place, next to him. A small basin rests in his lap. Today is Sunday, beard day. One razor-swipe at a time, with delicacy and precision. Not even the blade scraping over his face has the power to rouse my neighbor across the way. There's not a grimace of fear, of annoyance, nothing at all. With a towel, the father wipes away the residue of shaving cream. Alessandro is now perfectly clean-shaven. Now it's time for the hands. Like the shaving, the trimming of the nails proceeds slowly. For this operation, the father is aided by a pair of eyeglasses perched on his nose.

I had slept deeply, something not yet experienced during this mandatory stay. I arise with a specific aim, perhaps unwittingly imitating what I have just observed. In the big sack, my mother put a bit of everything, no doubt including a razor blade. Maybe I should pop in at the dispensary to tell them. In here, any kind of blade could provoke an Armageddon of sorts, like with Madonnina and the lighter he obtained from who knows where. But right now I just want to think of myself.

In the shower, I pare my face back up to the surface, buried under half a centimeter of facial hair that's tough as wire. The endeavor costs pain, which is added to my disgust for everything this bathroom contains, especially the sink and the shower stall. The white aluminum is full of black blisters, and rust tinges the water red. The desire to complete my project as soon as possible makes me rushed, but my beard does not allow me to go beyond a certain speed if I do not wish for every stroke of the blade to feel like a smack across the cheeks. Aftershave is kindly offered by Alessandro's father. Incredibly, my mother forgot it. When I see her again, I'll let her know—jokingly of course, although I don't think she will be in much of a mood for fun and games with me. I come out of the bathroom brand new.

Gianluca, just awake, looks at me greedily.

"Good morning. Damn, how'd you get so spiffy? You look like a different person." His voice is a whisper meant to seduce, at least that's what he's aiming for, but the look in my eye kills the temptress in him stone dead. And then Gianluca, the friend, is instantly back. His eyes blink and a crack appears on his face. His eyes disappear, swallowed up.

"I'm leaving today. I finished the mandatory commitment."

He should be jumping for joy, but he's crying. He hides his face in his hands. From in here, my life seems to me like a river of molten gold, of inestimable worth. For him, this blazing desert, our week of segregation, is the closest thing to happiness that occurs in his existence. I cannot imagine what awaits him out there, but it must be terrible—so terrible as to make an involuntary psychiatric treatment seem like a vacation, a fond memory to be cherished.

Giorgio, covered by the sheet way up over his head, is still sleeping deeply.

The same goes for Madonnina. He was moaning a lot, all night long. At a certain point I tried to calm him down. Then I sank into the kind of sleep I wish I could have for the rest of my life. Who knows what was tormenting him, what pain he was voicing. Maybe he, too, was wrestling with his past, provided that he still has the capacity to distinguish life in the past from life in the present and life in the future.

Mario is focused on his sparrow, but does not seem at all satisfied.

"I crumbled your cookie here on the windowsill, but he's not coming over. He can't overcome his fear." He answers my question before I have time to ask it.

Maybe I'm getting used to it, or maybe it's my shower-and-shave combo, but the heat seems more bearable today. The sky, which was whitish and heavy with mugginess, has recovered some of its deep blue.

I think of my folks at home. Sunday mornings are given over to domestic chores. I imagine my father is busy in the garden, mowing the lawn. My mother is housecleaning and preparing lunch. Tomorrow, all this will be mine again. I'll be taking back my life, my freedom.

Lorenzo looks in from the doorway. After my father's visit, he seems to have lost the ability to look me in the eye. He turns to Gianluca.

"Go to the doctor's office for a minute." Gianluca executes the order with the face of someone sentenced to death.

"Aren't you supposed to be off today?" I'm not actually interested in knowing why Lorenzo is on duty instead of being home or at the beach. It's just an attempt to re-establish a minimum amount of dialogue between us.

I am just as impulsive, inclined to overreact and be pugnacious as I am incapable of holding a grudge. Plus, I cannot tolerate the idea that someone might despise me.

"I'm getting married in six months, and we still have the whole house to furnish," Lorenzo answers.

He does not seem happy. I can't tell if it's for the sacrifice of working on a Sunday or for his future wedding. Pino with his lipless mouth comes to mind. He says that Lorenzo's fiancée smacks him around sometimes. But Pino's words must always be taken with a grain of salt.

Pleased as a man who has just hit the jackpot, his hands fluttering in delight, Gianluca returns to the room. Giorgio has just woken up and Madonnina is still half asleep. Gianluca plants a kiss on Giorgio's cheek first, then mine, then Madonnina's, then Mario's, and finally Alessandro's. Gianluca's kisses are loud and heartfelt.

"I was able to convince them! They're discharging me tomorrow!" He throws up his arms in triumph. Giorgio gets out of bed and imitates him. They embrace in the middle of the room. Mario and I look at each other amused. Gianluca's stay has filled everyone with cheer.

On television, Sunday Masses alternate with accusations levelled against the national team for losing the game last night. Neither interests me. Italia Uno is broadcasting *The Dukes of Hazzard*, but that's a series I never liked.

I remain at the window. The sea is once again visible on the horizon, confirming that the day is less sweltering than the preceding ones. I see before me the precise geometric lines of regimented fields, each devoted to a different crop, vineyards, small wooded zones—a sequence of colors and marvels. Lower in the picture are Pomezia and its hinterland, where the waste of big factories is climbing into the sky—it is just as marvelous and monumental.

For a long while I thought my eyes were diseased, as if a strange degeneration had given them a kind of loupe that made every vision something unique and enormous. Where others saw mere normalcy, I saw amazing wonders and unrepeatable events. Because of this mysterious illness, the achievements of other human beings took on an air of heroism, like my father's night shifts at the Atac transportation company, or the inexhaustible love in my mother's hands. Nature appeared to me as the queen of beauty, a treasure chest full of gems. All was immense, incredible. Over the years, I understood that I did not have an eye defect, but more likely a defect of the mind. All the way up to my twenty years of fire and brimstone. Now I know that it's not me, that I don't see things bigger than they are; I only see them in their real size. And things really are gigantic. Every single day is punctuated by deeds and visions worthy of an extraordinary epic—each person encountered, each new slice of reality. But I know that the awareness I now grip in my fists will pass, as it did in the past. Everything at that moment will go back to being the symptom of a still nameless derangement.

My life unfolds on a swing running amok.

I say these things to no one—like the yearning for salvation that overcomes me when pity breaks me. They are my secret, the part of me that is inaccessible to others.

The hospital kitchen has gifted us with white lasagna for our Sunday lunch. The appearance corresponds to the description, but the taste does not. With closed eyes, it could be anything at all. Of all the ingredients, not one remains on the palate, not one.

I finish about half, then start eating the fennel and tomato salad. After the layered nothingness of the lasagna, it is a concert of flavors. It's been almost a week since I've had coffee. I'd pay gold for a cup. Like many other wishes, this one will be met tomorrow. At least I hope so.

"Let's move it. I've got to clear this stuff away," shouts Pino, his genteel manner preceding his presence. Like Lorenzo, he hasn't let the Sunday shift pass him by. I look at him in his battle fatigues. His pants are a different white from his shirt, which is grayish. His feet are reliably shod in clogs.

"Weren't you supposed to stay home today?" I ask.

"Have any idea how much money the Sunday shift pays? Eighty thousand lire, got that? Eighty," he answers as he practically rips the plate from under Giorgio's chin as he was picking up the last bits of salad.

"So what does someone your age do with that money?" I query.

Pino stops dead in his tracks and glares at me like a bolt of lightning.

"Number one. Let's hope you even get to my age, 'cause looking at you now, it's far from certain. Number two. I'm fifty, not two hundred. Number three. Mind your own fucking business."

I deserved it. The question came out rude, and Pino didn't miss his chance. Perhaps moved by compassion, he pauses next to my bed. I think he likes me, in the end.

"Anyhow, given you asked me, even though you make me out to be an old man, I'll tell you. If all goes well, next year I'll be opening a fruit shop. My mother and father are greengrocers, and they still have their stand."

"Bravo," I say, really meaning it. He swells up, proud of the future he is creating for himself, one overtime after another.

Out in the corridor, Cimaroli rushes by in shorts and sandals. I hear him closing himself in the dispensary.

The phone at home rings and rings, but no one answers. I could bet my life that the picture is this: lunch outdoors under the gazebo my father erected with his own two hands, grilled meat, pastries for all.

"You're eating outside, right?" I ask.

I don't even know who picked up the phone.

"Of course, what with this heat." It's my brother.

"Where's Mamma?"

"She's outside. Here she is."

"Danie'?" I don't want to answer. My envy is mixed with jealousy, lots of it, an excessive amount, totally unjustified. Of course it's not my family's fault I'm in here.

"Everything good? All of you?" I end up asking.

EVERYTHING CALLS FOR SALVATION · 147

"Yes, Uncle Enzo came to see us." The news is a gracefully delivered kick in the teeth. I adore my uncle. His life would merit an encyclopedia, not under ten volumes.

"Great," I say.

"He knows everything about you. He said he'll come by next Sunday again so you can spend time together." The image of my family reunited with my uncle, all the extraordinary normality I'm missing out on, makes anger and bitterness rise up to my throat. But I don't want my mother to notice.

"Did anyone ask for me?"

"Yes, Marco and Giuliano. I said you were away for a week because you had found a small job."

"Good. Remember, don't tell anyone anything."

"You can count on me."

"Say hi to uncle."

If my friends knew my real whereabouts and the reason I was here, I'd quite simply be ruined. I'd lose everything.

This realization only serves to fill the moment with more gall. Except for my family members, who know it and endure it, no one else is aware of my true nature. Doctors don't count, of course.

In reality, though, there are some others.

It doesn't hit me until now.

They are the five crazies with whom I'm sharing the room and one week of my life.

With them, I did not have the possibility to lie, to recite the role of the perfect person. They have accepted me for what I am, for my nature, so close to theirs.

With them, I've been talking about illness, God and death, time and beauty, without feeling judged or analyzed.

This had never happened to me before.

These five crazies are the closest thing to friendship I've ever encountered—more, even, they're like brothers offered by life, found in the same boat in the middle of the same storm, caught between lunacy and some other thing that one day I'll be able to name.

From the corridor I stop and take a look at them.

There they are, each in his own corner of the room, defenselessly facing their own condition, exposed to the weather, naked men clinging to life, crushed by an insanity handed to them.

My brothers.

Sunday afternoon is a slow-motion movie of a billiard ball being knocked from nowhere to nowhere. Tomorrow at this hour I'll be out of here, I'll have my life back, finally. I smile to myself, try to cheer myself up, but it is not what I really feel. I'm afraid. Going back to life means going back to the job I abandoned. It means taking up the discussion about my future. What future?

What can I expect? With this head I carry on my shoulders, how will I turn out? I'd like to give myself a thousand answers, but in truth I do not grant myself even one. What destiny can someone have who transforms even happiness into suffering?

Mario is stretching way out the window, trying to place a piece of cookie directly in the bird's nest.

If he's not careful.

A thump in the garden.

Mario has fallen.

Mario fell from the window.

I turn to the others.

Gianluca and Giorgio saw it like me.

"He fell," I say, at least I think I did.

In Gianluca's eyes I see the girl inside him going ballistic.

A chilling scream. It's infinite.

Giorgio has covered his eyes with his hands.

"Mario! Mario fell!" Gianluca shrieks like a possessed girl. He tears at his hair. Giorgio jumps up on his bed. A kind of low howl comes from his mouth.

My God.

Pino enters the room, scans it without understanding, then strides to the window, looks down, one hand on his mouth, then both on his eyes.

Cimaroli joins him, looks out. His whole body seems to recoil, as if from a gun-shot. He grabs Pino by the arm, then he runs off.

I do not have the guts to go see.

My God.

Pino goes to Gianluca, takes him by the shoulders, shakes him to calm him down, once, twice, but there is no way.

"Shut up!"

He yells so loud he needs to grasp the bed-head. He regains his composure after a kind of dizzy spell.

Silence.

Only the breathing of animals.

I look over at Madonnina, but he has disappeared.

Alessandro has not moved his eyes from his spot.

My God.

"Now you keep still, shut up, don't move. Understand?" No one answers Pino, but not a voice is heard, no movement is made.

He returns to the window, looks down for a long while. Agitated voices travel up. Shouts.

"They've taken him away."

I can't see my own face, but Gianluca's is terrified, Giorgio's is a mask of sweat. His eyes are frantic, darting distraughtly.

I drink some water. I'm in the bathroom, then in the hallway, just like the others. We're roaming around like whirling dervishes, mute.

Cimaroli comes back to the ward, requesting that we enter our room.

"Everybody on their own bed, please."

We comply instantly.

"He is here in the emergency room. He's critical. Now, calm down. We'll all calm down and wait. Is that clear?"

I discharge all the tears I can on my pillow.

Every single smile.

Every single gesture of extreme kindness.

Visions of Mario hit me like a whip.

His rumpled pajamas.

The baked apples in small bites.

For Gianluca and Giorgio, too, the time has come for tears.

"I've lost my soul, Mary! Help me, my little Madonna!"

Giorgio stares at Madonnina, and then, as if he had gone raving mad, he gets off his bed, grabs me by an arm, pulls me to the middle of the room and leaves me there. He does the same thing with Gianluca.

Now the three of us are close together.

Giorgio kneels.

"Let us pray."

He offers his hands to us. Gianluca and I are taken aback, but then we grasp one another's hand. The three of us kneel.

Giorgio makes the sign of the cross. We copy him.

"Jesus, Joseph and Mary, help Mario, don't let him die. Give your grace to him and to us. We love him because he is good. Amen."

His eyes invite Gianluca to continue.

"Our Father who art in heaven, help Mario, make him live, we pray to you with all our heart, because in my life, I have known few people as good as he."

Gianluca's eyes pass the baton to me.

How to start? What to say?

"God I pray to you, I pray that you want to protect Mario for all he has suffered, because all the evil did not make him mean. He listened to everybody, and always had a kind word for everyone. I pray to you God."

After the words, it's time to share tears.

They are passed from Giorgio to Gianluca to me.

A harried Mancino looks in from the doorway, immediately joined by Cimaroli. The two enter our room as we heave ourselves up off the floor.

"He was trying to feed a little bird," I announce to both, but they seem to not hear me.

"Have there been any suicide attempts in his medical history?" Mancino is not asking us, but Cimaroli.

"No. He was charged with injuring his wife, but suicide attempts don't seem to be part of the picture."

"He fell. He didn't jump, you know. We saw it, all three of us," says Gianluca.

He has better luck than I. Mancino and Cimaroli notice his words, but don't react. They both leave the room.

"I've lost my soul, Mary! Help me, my little Madonna!"

Giorgio takes our hands again. He falls down on his knees heavily, and we follow suit.

"Jesus, Joseph and Mary, give Mario grace. Make him come back to us here."

The sky darkens as the evening wears on.

Three or four hours have passed.

They tried to serve us dinner, but all of us refused.

We run out of our room in search of news every time there's a buzz at the door to the ward, or the telephone rings.

But news does not come.

Even the head physician drops by the ward. Like Mancino, he had been called in because of the tragedy. He remains for a few minutes, speaks to Cimaroli and Pino, then vanishes.

I look at Gianluca. He's spent. Not a wisp of energy is left in his eyes. Agony is a beast slipped under our skin. I take his hand and squeeze it.

"You should have left this morning," I try to make him smile. He makes an attempt, to no avail.

Giorgio sits like a big creature all curled up. Every so often he raises his head sunken between his knees, then drops it back in.

Evening turns into night.

The telephone rings. Cimaroli's shapeless voice speaks. As much as I try, I cannot hear what he says.

The door of the doctors' office opens. It's Cimaroli, and he walks toward us.

"Good news."

His smile is a miraculous medicine.

The fatigue lifts. Now there are liberating tears of joy, hugs, kisses.

"They stopped the internal hemorrhaging. He has some broken bones, but is no longer in critical condition. He's conscious, too. As soon as he stabilizes, they'll take him to Rome. Unfortunately, there's no room here."

Giorgio joins his hands at the center of his chest and lifts his gaze to the lamp planted in the ceiling.

"Jesus, Joseph and Mary, thank you for Mario. Amen."

He looks at us. It's a silent order.

"Thank you Jesus," I say.

"Our Father who art in heaven, thank you for Mario," says Gianluca.

Cimaroli opens his arms toward us.

"Now you all go to bed, it's time to rest and sleep."

Slowly, his arms still open, he comes toward us, as if to herd us toward our beds.

"Doctor, could we go say a little hello? Daniele and I are leaving tomorrow morning, so we might not see Mario anymore," Gianluca attempts.

Cimaroli listens comprehensively.

"I realize that, but as you can imagine, it is really not possible.

They have put him in intensive care. Plus, you are patients. You can't wander around the hospital. Lastly, all three of you are in mandatory confinement."

"But just one little hello. We say 'ciao,' wave our hand, and leave."

Gianluca's new attempt shatters against Cimaroli's polite but tight smile.

"No, you cannot. Now get to bed."

"This time you're going to let me see her. This time, yes," Giorgio's breathing is becoming labored.

I turn toward him.

It all becomes clear: what is happening here, and what he is turning in to, right now, next to me.

I look at Cimaroli, try to catch his eye to make him understand. Gianluca does not seem to have registered anything.

But Cimaroli does not pick up on it. He's blind.

"Now please get into bed," he entreats.

His polite smile has evaporated.

"You let me see her right now! Immediately!"

Giorgio grows like bread dough during the night, like children over the years, like grass under the sun. He grows in height and width, out of rage.

"Go to your bed this instant!" shouts Cimaroli.

All the laws of physics suddenly fly out the window.

Cimaroli's body becomes as light as a paper airplane shoved into the air.

Giorgio has taken him by the chest with his hands and tossed him off, just like that.

Cimaroli crashes into our lockers.

I look at Gianluca. He's expressionless, as if paralyzed, like Alessandro, like a statue of flesh.

Giorgio turns to us.

"I don't want to be nasty."

The last flicker of himself drowns in the black of his eyes.

"What the hell did you do?!" Pino enters and confronts him.

"What the hell did you—"

Giorgio's clenched fists land soundly in the middle of his chest. Pino falls to the ground, looking at us without making sense of it. Then an expression of pain floods his scarred face.

"Giorgio, please, calm down, calm down," Gianluca says crying. He stretches out his arms in an attempt to placate him, but Giorgio is no longer there. He has been swallowed by this other being now in front of us.

"Don't touch me!" he yells.

I grab Gianluca by the arm, and retreat with him until we arrive at the wall on the far side of my bed, next to Alessandro.

Two nurses arrive from the door, having heard the shouting.

"Knock it off! Settle down!" they say.

Giorgio lowers his head slightly, then plows into them. All three are sprawled on the floor, with him on top. His arms like boulders are pounding their faces. The nurses have no time to react.

I urge Gianluca to do like me, bend down, hide.

Across from us, underneath the bed beside the lockers, Cimaroli lies spread out with his hands on his ears, his eyes open wide. Pino is still in the middle of the room. He looks like he's saying words, like he's asking something.

My God.

Who is crazy? Who is sane?

Giorgio lifts himself up off the nurses; his face is a mask of crooked features looking for oxygen.

Mancino is at the door.

He looks at Giorgio hard.

He walks toward him, one step at a time, his eyes glued to Giorgio's.

Giorgio charges.

The violent crunch of two bodies colliding head-on.

Mancino is able to enclose Giorgio's upper body, pinning his arms. His exertion is clenched between his teeth. He holds Giorgio there, gripping him so tight to take away his breath.

Giorgio tries to wiggle out. With extreme force, he tries to make Mancino fall backward, but Mancino resists.

Mancino turns his face toward us.

His eyes are marked by exhaustion. They shine with pity and tears.

They remain fixed in that hold, two equal forces opposing each other.

"Why didn't you let me see her? Why?"

Giorgio's weeping starts soaking up his rage.

His crying is centuries old.

He cries without strength, spent.

Mancino lets him go, but remains at his side.

He begins caressing him, like fathers do to their frightened children. He welcomes Giorgio into his arms as if their blood were one.

Gianluca and I look at each other without saying anything. We are survivors, rescued from the war, without joy, without even the strength to wish for something.

They take us and lock us up in the dispensary.

Gianluca, Madonnina and me.

I no longer have the faculty of judging time—neither past time nor the time we are spending closed in here.

Gianluca and Madonnina are both sleeping on the same cot.

I am sitting on a chair fiddling with a roll of gauze.

The door opens.

It's Cimaroli.

Without a word, he brings us back to the room.

Giorgio is no longer there.

Neither is Mancino, nor Pino, nor the nurses.

Gianluca and Madonnina are exhausted. They collapse on their mattresses.

I remain focused on Cimaroli.

"Please give me something to sleep," I ask.

Without a reaction, he walks off.

When he comes back, his trembling hands offer me an entire blister pack of Phenegran.

I swallow three.

I lie down in bed and immediately notice what's new.

Something about the battle of giants seems to have penetrated Alessandro's world.

He no longer looks toward a point half a meter above my head.

Now he is fully lying down on the bed. His eyes are still open, but now aimed at a precise spot on the ceiling.

Day 7
Monday

"I've lost my soul, Mary! Help me, my little Madonna!"

Black and more black. This must be death.

I feel like a hand is pressing on my eyelids, a mighty hand, like Giorgio's. My head is struggling. It is incredulous of the memories bubbling up.

It did happen. It's all true.

Finally I succeed in opening my eyes.

One pill of Phenegran, and you wake up bright-eyed and bushy-tailed. But if you take three, you're in for a nasty wallop.

It takes me a while to regain my composure, remember my first name, my last name, my life. Then my eyes run to see what is left of my roommates.

Mario's bed has been made up; the nightstand has been cleared. His paltry belongings and the bottle filled with tap-water from the bathroom are all gone. You couldn't even tell that Mario ever lived in that corner or crashed down from that window just a fistful of hours ago.

That was his magic enclosure. That was where he took me in. It's where we spoke.

Also the bed to my right has been made up. Where could Giorgio be? Is he well? Let's hope he acquires some self-control, and that no one provokes him. Like Mario's, his space contains not a trace of his person or the event.

I do not know how long I have slept, but judging from the

temperature of the tea in the cup, I'd say that breakfast has been over for quite some time. It's probably after nine o'clock, maybe ten.

On Gianluca's bed lies a closed bag. His nightstand has been emptied, too.

"I've lost my soul, Mary! Help me, my little Madonna!"

At least Madonnina has stayed in his place.

As has Alessandro. Someone, maybe he himself, has put him back in the original position. Now he is staring at the same spot again, half a meter above my head, where it always used to be.

The door of the doctors' office opens and Gianluca enters our room, with his mother in tow. I rise from the bed. The Phenegran continues to slow me down and muddle my every movement.

Gianluca has a tough time raising his eyes from the ground. He is no longer wearing his pajama shorts hiked up high to reveal as much of his hairy thighs as possible. He is dressed in a pair of skinny jeans and a T-shirt printed with a kitten licking its paw. His mother stays put at the door.

Gianluca walks over to me.

His embrace is brief; his mother's gaze is fixed upon us.

He forces a smile, but the tears are irrepressible. He makes a superhuman effort to speak:

"Don't tell me we'll see each other again."

I shake my head, "No."

Each of us takes the face of the other into his hands. We stay looking at each other, engraving the moment on our memory.

Gianluca breaks away, goes toward his bed, grabs the handles of his overnight bag and swings it over his shoulder.

He disappears, followed closely by his mother.

I have to lie down.

Uselessly, I order myself to resist. Then I ask myself why.

I let the pain pierce me, let the tears drag me away.

At the door stands a nurse I haven't seen before. He notices the state I'm in.

"Your turn in the doctors' office for discharge," he says to me.

He lingers, studying the room, seeming to wonder. Yes, it all happened precisely here.

In the doctors' office I find Cimaroli. Next to him stands the head physician.

"How is Mario? What about Giorgio?" I ask.

"They brought Mario to San Camillo hospital early this morning. He's doing well, the hemorrhage is under control. His right leg is badly broken, he's going to need an operation. Giorgio was taken to the psychiatric ward at the Velletri penitentiary," says the head physician. Cimaroli prefers not to look at me.

"What do you mean, the Velletri penitentiary?" I ask.

"He attacked the doctors and nurses. We had no choice," he answers.

"What about Pino? How's Pino?"

"He has a broken rib. He'll be back when it heals. The two nurses will be off duty for about ten days."

They all come to life in my mind's eye.

Those poor nurses, who came running toward the shouts without this even being their ward.

Pino, at home in pain, cooped up with his rudeness, his dream of Rossana and everything that could have been, his plan for the fruit stand that will liberate him from

this infernal drudgery forever.

Mario, immobile in his room at San Camillo, at war with the pain in his body, as if the old pains in his mind, under his tousled curls, were not enough. I think of him and the precious humanity he has to offer the universe.

And lastly Giorgio, locked up in a room behind bars, falling apart from loneliness, finding space on his shoulder for the umpteenth cut, the latest notch to remind him and the world of the visit with his mother, denied, just as the visit with Mario was.

"You could have let us see him for one second, just to say hi. Then none of this would have happened," I say to Cimaroli.

Rage is burning on my face, up to my ears. With effort, he raises his eyes to look at me.

"So. On this day 20 June 1994, you have concluded the mandatory psychiatric commitment requested on 13 June. We have informed by fax your local municipality and the court of Velletri of the end of your detention."

I keep staring at him. It is the same man who crawled under a bed last night with his hands over his ears. He takes another sheet of paper from the medical records and clears his throat.

"Based on the conducted consultations and your clinical history, we have decided to discharge you with a diagnosis of major depression. As I mentioned to you a few days ago, your pharmacological treatment is based on 60 milligrams daily of paroxetine, an antidepressant of the selective serotonin reuptake inhibitor class. You will start with 20 milligrams for one week, then 40 milligrams for another week, then 60 milligrams."

He swivels the paper toward me and passes me the pen.

"Sign here for your release," he says.

I execute the order.

"Say hello to Mancino. Give him my thanks."

Cimaroli does not answer. He closes me up in the medical folder marked with my name. As far as he is concerned, all of me is in there.

The head physician stretches out his hand. I shake it.

"Take care," he says.

I throw my things in my bag randomly. In my heart there is no more rage but resignation, overflowing bitterness. I snatch my jeans, my T-shirt from the locker. Dried blood stains everywhere. My blood. Marks of the night of madness that brought me here.

Mario's personal effects are still in the bathroom, plus Giorgio's toothbrush. I take what belongs to me—soap, razor, towels—and shove it all in the garbage can. I pause to stare at myself in the mirror. I command myself joy. I'll be out of here in a little bit, out of this futile nightmare. But no joy comes.

I give my nightstand a last once-over. I bend down and check under the bed. Nothing of mine is left in this place.

Mario's window is still open, as it always was.

I mosey over and look out. I lean my elbows on the sill where his were yesterday. The pieces of cookie are still where he put them out for his friend. I gave him those cookies. The bird's nest is empty now.

It would have taken so little.

It would have sufficed to listen, look in his eyes, grant him what he wanted.

Once, just for once.

But they didn't do it.

Because to them, we were not worthy of being listened to.

Because the crazies and the sickos need treatment, while words and dialogue are reserved for healthy people.

Is this dehumanization called science?

No compassion, just emptying a person until they're a thing of mere flesh, lording it over them as if they had all the answers.

Is this normality? Is this mental health?

True craziness is never giving up, never bowing to them.

One week ago, I wanted to kill life for its total lack of logic, for my certainty that nothing is foreseeable, that my cursed lot is to live without ever getting used to life, to any of it, whether good or bad.

I will live unhappily. Sooner or later, my suffering will gain ground, but I do not want to become like you.

Out of the blue, with its glittery black eyes, the sparrow returns to its house of twigs and leaves. I greet it on behalf of Mario.

I stop at Alessandro's bed. I'm not good at prayers, but not too shabby with my imagination. May this cocoon of silence soon be broken. May you return to this earth. Liberated.

Madonnina stands next to his bed, motionless. He is busy observing something in the void that is visible only to him. I go over and touch his hand lightly.

"Ciao, Madonni'," I say.

I lift my bag, giving the room one last glance.

I poke my head into the dispensary, trying to find a nurse with whom to entrust my regards for Pino, Rossana and Lorenzo, but no one is there.

"I've lost my soul, Mary! Help me, my little Madonna!"

I run into Madonnina in the hallway.

I can't be sure, but I see something in his eyes. Maybe they light up because I want them to, but there in the lasting darkness is a glimmer of light directed at me.

"I've lost my soul, Mary! Help me, my little Madonna!"

I embrace it all.

The stink of urine mixed with sweat, the worn-out bones, the prickly beard.

I hug everything about Madonnina, right down to the marrow—the concealed glory, the promised joy. Until the tears come, making me a man.

I did not ask anyone to come fetch me. I want to walk, breathe, be out in the air on my own. My legs have a hard time, no longer used to their task. The enormity of everything—the space, the colors—bedazzles and beguiles. Beauty conquers my eyes.

I halt to catch my breath. For just one second, I look back.

From on high, from the extremities of the universe, passing at the speed of light through my skull and down to my heels and beyond, traversing each atom of matter, everything is asking me for salvation.

For the living and for the dead: salvation.

For Mario, Gianluca, Giorgio, Alessandro and Madonnina: salvation.

For all the crazies there have ever been, swallowed by the nuthouses of history.

ACKNOWLEDGEMENTS

To the doctors in every corner of the world who place science hand in hand with love.

To Giovanni, Marilena, Francesco, Alessia, Camilla, Mara, Alice, Chiara and Mario—friends, companions in an adventure between life and books. You are Mondadori.

To Maria Cristina for her invincible enthusiasm and endless listening.

To my family, because it will take a thousand books to settle my account.

To Rina, Elena and all mothers who took me in in addition to mine.

To Nameless, Pietro, Francesco at the end, to children without faces who give flesh to hope.

To everybody who was able to pardon me.

To everybody I was unable to pardon.